# A
# BOOK OF FOLK-LORE

Rev. S. BARING-GOULD, M.A.

DETROIT • 1970
**Singing Tree Press**

This is a facsimile reprint of the 1913
edition published by W. Collins & Co. Ltd.,
London.

Library of Congress Catalog Card Number 69-16807

# CONTENTS

# A Book of Folk-Lore

## CHAPTER I

### PRELIMINARY

In the early days of exploration of prehistoric relics little care was bestowed on discriminating the several layers of deposit through which the spade cut, and what was found was thrown up into a common heap, and little account was taken as to the depths at which the several deposits lay.

I had the chance in 1892 of visiting La Laugerie Basse on the Vézère in company with Dr Massénat and M. Philibert Lalande, who conducted the exploration after MM. Christy and Lartet had abandoned the field. They had to carry on the work with very limited means, but they arrived, nevertheless, at conclusions which had escaped the earlier explorers.

Dr Massénat had driven a shaft down beside the bed of the peasant who lived under the rock, and who, when I saw him, was bed-ridden. His children, pretty brown-eyed boys and girls, bare-footed and bare-legged, were there, and I gave them some sous. As the dwelling was under the rock and the floor was earth, the refuse of the meals of the family went to raise the deposit along with particles of chalk falling from above. One of my sous, bearing the effigy of Napoleon III., fell, and in the scuffle that ensued disappeared under the soil. By the sick man's bed, as already stated, was a shaft driven down to the virgin soil, and this passed through a layer very modern, in which to this day my sou lies, then through fragments of Mediæval crockery, next Merovingian relics, then Roman scraps of iron and coins, below that remains of the Bronze Age, below that again those of the Polished Stone Period. Then ensued a gap—a tract of sterile soil; and then all at once began a rich bed of deposits—this time distinct from the rest in that they pertained to a people who were contemporary with the mammoth, the cave-bear, and the reindeer in France. Finally in this lay the skeleton of a man whose thigh had been crushed by a fallen mass of stone from the rock that arched over it, and who had been clothed in skins ornamented with shells from the Atlantic coast.

From this it may be seen how important

it is to differentiate the strata at which lie the remains of ancient man.

The same may be said with regard to folk-lore. A great amount had been collected into heaps, but no attempt had been made on a large scale to sift and sort out what had been found, and determine to what layer in our population they belong. The grouping is of the crudest. Birth, marriage, death lore go into their several piles, so do ghost and witch stories, and tales of dwarfs. What we really want to know is, Whence came the several items found?

Here, in Great Britain, we form an amalgam of several distinct races, and each race has contributed something towards the common stock of folk-lore. In my own neighbourhood we have two distinct types of humanity: one with high cheek-bones, dusky skin, dark hair, full of energy, unscrupulous as to the *meum* and *tuum*, money-making, by every conceivable means. The other is fair-haired, clear-skinned, slow, steady, honourable, with none of the alertness of the other. I can point out a family: the eldest girl, illegitimate, is wild, indisciplinable, dark-haired and sallow-skinned, The mother, of the same type, married a fair-haired man, and the children are of mixed breed.

Through intermarriage there is an importation of the superstitious beliefs of the lower type into the higher. This has been going on for a long time. A dominating race absorbs some of the convictions of the race it has subdued; and we generally find that the former regard the latter with some awe, as possessed of magical and mysterious powers beyond its own range of acquisitions.

We cannot say that a certain bit of folklore is Celtic and not pre-Celtic because picked up where there is fusion of blood, any more than we can say that a piece of granite strewed upon alluvial soil or lying on limestone belongs to that on which it rests.

Mr Tyler and Sir J. Fraser, the great students in Comparative Folk-lore, have devoted their attention to the development and expansion of certain primitive beliefs and practices, but Mr Gomme, in his epoch-making book, *Ethnology in Folk-lore* (London, 1892), was the first to my knowledge who pointed out the necessity of classification according to the beds whence the items of folk-lore came.

In this volume, which does not pretend to be more than a popular introduction to the study of the science, I have confined myself as much as possible to the beliefs of the peoples who occupied the British Isles, and have not gone like other writers to the usages of savages for explanation of customs and traditions, except very occasionally.

In some instances we can trace scraps of folk-lore back to whence they came. In the legends of several of the Irish saints we have them represented as floating over the sea on leaves. The idea is so odd and so preposterous —as there are in Ireland no leaves of any size that could be serviceable—that we are constrained to look back and see whether this be not an adaptation of a much earlier myth. Now, in an old Flemish poem on Brandæin, or St Brendan the Voyager, he meets on the ocean with a Thumbling seated on a leaf, floating, in one hand a pan, in the other a style. This latter he dipped into the sea, and from it let drops trickle into the pan. When the vessel was full he emptied it and renewed the process, and this he is condemned to continue doing till he has drained the ocean dry. Whence came this fantastic conception? It was brought from the original seats of the Aryan people in the East, for there Brahma is represented as floating over the deep on a lotus. And after the death of Brahma, when water overflowed the whole earth, then Vischnu sat, as a small child, on a fig-leaf,

and floated on the wild sea, sucking the toe
of his right foot.

In a wild and upland district in East Cornwall is the ancient mansion of the Trevelyans.
It comprises a quadrangle with granite
mullioned windows, and is entered through
a handsome gate-house. At the time of the
Commonwealth, here lived a Squire Peter
Trevelyan; he was born in 1613 and died in
1705—there is nothing like being precise. He
was a staunch Royalist, and a band of Round-
head soldiers was sent to arrest him. They
came to the gate-house and rapped. Squire
Trevelyan put his head out of the window
above—they show you the very window to
this day—and bade the crop-eared rascals be
off, or he would send his lance-men after
them and forcibly dislodge them. As they
did not stir, he took a couple of bee-hives he
had in the chamber over the gate and flung
them among the troopers. The bees swarmed
out, fell on and speedily dispersed them.

Andernach, on the Rhine, was engaged in
incessant feud with the town of Linz; and one
night it was attacked by the citizens of the
rival town. The watchmen were asleep, so
also the townsfolk; but two bakers' apprentices were engaged at the oven, when, hearing
a sound outside the walls, they mounted to

the parapets and saw the enemy engaged in planting ladders. Instantly they caught up some bee-hives that were on the walls and flung them among the assailants. The bees rushed out, and proved such terrible *lanz-knects* that the Linzers were routed and sent flying helter-skelter home. Can the story be doubted? The citizens of Andernach point to the figures of the two youths carved in stone at one of the portals, and tell you that this was done in acknowledgment of their achievement.

At Ballyrawney in Ireland a story is told to this effect. About eight centuries ago a powerful chief, on the point of waging war against the head of another clan, seeing the inferiority of his troops, begged St Gobnat to assist him, and this was in a field near where the battle was about to be fought. In this field was a bee-hive, and the saint granted the request by turning the bees into spearmen, who issued from the hive with all the ardour of warriors, fell on the enemy, and put him to rout. After the battle the conquering chief revisited the spot whence he had received such miraculous aid, when he found that the straw hive had been metamorphosed into an article shaped like a helmet and composed of brass. This relic remains to this day in testimony to the truth of the story, and is in the possession of the O'Hierlyhie family, and is held by the Irish peasantry in such profound veneration that they will travel several miles to procure a drop of water from it, which, if given to a dying relative or friend, they imagine will secure their sure admission into heaven.    Crofton Croker, who tells this story, adds that not long ago some water from this brazen bee-hive was administered to a dying priest by his coadjutor, in compliance with the popular superstition.

These stories were not wafted from one place to another, but derived from a common origin when the bees were regarded as friends and protectors of a house or a town.    They went by the name of 'the Birds of God,' or 'Mary's birds' in Germany, and were supposed to be in communication with the Spirit. When a master died in a house, his heir went before the hive and announced the death to the bees and entreated them to remain and protect him.    In like manner, when a young couple became engaged they informed the bees and requested their favour.    To some extent they would seem to have been regarded as the household spirits guarding a family, and they were always treated with reverence. A hive might never be sold, only given.

Now that we have sugar supplied so freely, we can hardly realise to what an extent honey was formerly required, not only for sweetening cakes, but also for the brewing of metheglin, or mead.  It was the drink of the gods; and if a child was to be cast out to die, if a compassionate neighbour touched its lips with honey the heathen father dare not allow it to perish.  This occurs in the life of St Liudger, whose mother Liafburg was saved by this means when the father had ordered her to be drowned.

There be certain superstitions not easy to be explained.  Actors and actresses have a strong prejudice against performing in green dresses.  I once heard a cultured man in Yorkshire explain, quite seriously, that the disturbed condition in pre-war England, the strikes, the labour unrest, and suffragist outrages, were due to the introduction of the green halfpenny stamp; and green throughout England and Scotland is regarded as an unlucky colour.  Mr Henderson, in his *Northern Folk-lore*, says : 'Green, ever an ominous colour in the Lowlands of Scotland, must on no account be worn at a wedding.  The fairies, whose chosen colour it is, would resent the insult and destroy the wearer.  Whether on this account or on any other I know not,

but the notion of ill-luck in connection with
it is widespread.  I have heard of mothers in
the South of England who absolutely forbade
their daughters to wear anything of this
colour, and who avoided it even in the furni-
ture of their homes.'  The real reason is that
green being the colour of the elves and pixies,
if worn gives these imps a power over those
who have assumed their colour; and renders
the bride in 'gown of green' liable to be
carried off to one of their underground
abodes.

There is a very curious story told by
William of Newburgh, who was born in the
reign of King Stephen, and wrote his *Chronicle*
down to 1198; it is also found in Radulf of
Coggeshall, who wrote his *English History* in
1223.

In Suffolk, at Woolpit (wolf-pits originally),
near Stowmarket, a boy and his sister were
found by the inhabitants of that place near
the mouth of a pit.  They were formed like
other children, but the whole of their skin was
of a green colour.  No one could understand
their speech.  When they were brought as
curiosities to the house of Sir Richard de
Calne, at Wikes, they wept bitterly.  Bread
and other victuals were set before them, but
they would not touch them.  At length, when

some beans just cut, with their stalks, were brought into the house, they made signs with great avidity that they should be given to them. When they were brought, they opened the stalks instead of the pods, thinking the beans were in the hollow of them; but not finding them, they wept anew. When those who were present saw this, they opened the pods and showed them the naked beans. They fed on these with great delight, and for a long time tasted no other food. The boy, however, was always languid and depressed, and he died within a short time. The girl enjoyed constant good health; and becoming accustomed to various kinds of food, lost completely that green colour, and gradually recovered the sanguine habit of her whole body. She was afterwards baptized, and lived for many years in the service of the knight, but was rather loose and wanton in her conduct. William of Newburgh says that he long hesitated to believe the story, but was at length overcome by the weight of evidence. At length the girl married a man at Lenna (Lynn?), and lived many years. She told that she and her brother came from an underground land where there was no sun, but enjoyed a degree of light like twilight in summer. Whatever credence may be put in her story,

F.-L.                                                      B it seems that there is some truth in the tale, and that these two children belonged to the Elfin or Dwarf stock that still lingered in the land. The green hue is probably an addition, so as to make them of Fairy stock. One can see now that there was a reason for the prejudice against green as being the colour of the strange people so far below the Aryan occupants of the land in intellect and culture.

That some of the myths of dwarfs 'are connected with traditions of real indigenous or hostile tribes is settled beyond question by the evidence brought forward by Grimm, Nilsson, and Hanusch. With all the difficulty of analysing the mixed nature of the dwarfs of European folk-lore, and judging how far they are elves, or gnomes, or such like nature spirits, and how far human beings in a mystic aspect, it is impossible not to recognise this latter element in the kindly or mischievous aborigines of the land, with their special language, and religion, and costume.'[1]

As a farmer marks his sheep, and his horse turned out on the moors by a hole punched in the ear, or a snip, so persons are marked out as pertaining to the gods. Circumcision marks as pertaining to Jehovah or to Allah. The tonsure marks the priest or monk as belonging

[1] Tylor (E. B.). *Primitive Culture*, 1871, I. 348.

to God; and the green colour worn is a sign that the person or thing so indicated is given over to the Elves.

In trying to allot the various superstitions dealt with in these pages, it must be borne in mind that we have to do with a pre-Aryan people, as well as Aryan people who had long passed out of the earliest and the rudest forms of myth-making and ceremonial, and animistic beliefs. They brought their convictions with them to our island, but in a modified form; and the modifications were due either to advance in culture or to contact with other peoples whose opinions were different from their own. Moreover, each stock, pre-Aryan and Aryan, brought with it some elements that pertained to a condition of mind and belief that had been common to both, but out of which both had grown.

The field of folk-lore is so extensive and so interesting, that it cannot be ploughed up by one hand and its riches revealed. All that I have attempted to do is to take a few salient points in it and show to what conclusions they lead, and as far as might be I have drawn on my own experience in collecting the folk-lore of the West of England.

## CHAPTER II

### THE SPIRIT OF MAN

THERE is a remarkable Arabian story called *Hai Ebn Yokdhan*, written in Spain by Ebn Tophail. It is a philosophical romance, and relates how a child brought up by a nanny-goat began to study the secrets of life. His nurse, the goat, died, and he wondered in what existed the spring of life, and he cut her open and searched the heart, where he found two compartments, one filled with coagulated blood, the other empty. From that he was led to search into what the vacant cavity once contained. He slew a goat, cut it open, and found in the vacant cavity a vaporous bluish flame—and that was Life.

Life is light and fire. This idea must have entered into the minds of primitive people. To this day in Yorkshire falling stars are supposed to be the souls coming down from above to new-born children and animating them, and when death ensues the flame of life passes out of the body. This is the conception that lies at the root of many folk-superstitions.

I knew a case in an adjoining parish,

where there was a young man in a decline who had helped in the hay-harvest. He was dead before the next season. But I was assured that at haysel a flame was seen dancing about the meadow and running up to the hayrick; the haymakers had no doubt whatever that this was the spirit of the young man who had died in the previous year. In Wales the belief in corpse-lights is very prevalent. There it is a flame that comes from the churchyard to fetch the spirit of the dying man or woman. It is, in fact, the spirit of a relative come to call it.

It is called the Canwyll Gorph, or Corpse Candle; and the saying is that St David promised to Welshmen in his territory that none should die without the premonitory sign of a light travelling to his house from the churchyard to summon him. In the *Cambrian Register* for 1796 we read of—

A very commonly received opinion, that within the diocese of St David's, a short space before death, a light is seen proceeding from the house, and sometimes, as has been asserted, from the very bed where the sick person lies, and pursues its way to the church where he or she is to be interred, precisely in the same track in which the funeral is afterwards to follow.

In Devonshire it is supposed that this light is only seen when the moribund has children or relatives buried in the churchyard, and it is the souls of these that come to fetch their kinsman or kinswoman.

All under the stars, and beneath the green tree,
All over the sward, and along the cold lea,
    A little blue flame a-fluttering came;
It came from the churchyard for you or for me.

I sit by the cradle, my baby's asleep,
And rocking the cradle, I wonder and weep.
    O little blue light in the dead of the night,
O prithee, O prithee, no nearer to creep.

Why follow the church-path, why steal you this
        way?
Why halt in your journey, on threshold why
        stay?
    With flicker and flare, why dance up the stair?
O I would! O I would! it were dawning of day.

All under the stars, and along the green lane,
Unslaked by the dew, and unquenched by the
        rain,
    Of little flames blue to the churchyard steal two.
The soul of my baby! now from me is ta'en.

Baxter, in his *Certainty of the World of Spirits*, quotes a letter from Mr John Davis of Gleneurglyn, 1656, in which he says that the corpse-candles do as much resemble material candle-light as eggs do eggs, saving that in their journey these candles are sometimes visible and sometimes disappear, especially if any one comes near them, or in any way meet them. On these occasions they vanish, but presently appear again. If a little candle is seen of a pale bluish colour, then follows the corpse of an infant; if a larger one, then the corpse of some one come to age. If two candles come from different places and be seen to meet, the corpses will do the same; and if any of these candles be seen to turn aside through some bypath leading to the church, the following corpse will be found to take exactly the same way. The belief in Devonshire is very much the same as that in Wales, only it is held that no corpse-candle will come to fetch a soul unless there be a kinsman already interred in the churchyard.

That there may be an amount of gas that is luminous escaping from a tomb is possible enough. I had one night dining with me a friend who is now a vice-principal of a college in Oxford. To reach his home he had to pass our churchyard, and he came back in terror as he had seen a blue light dancing above a grave. But that these flames should travel down roads and seek houses where there is one dying is, of course, an exaggeration and untenable.

Baxter tells the story of what happened at Llangatten in Carmarthenshire :—

Some thirty or forty years since my wife's sister, being nurse to Bishop Rudd's three eldest children, the lady comptroller of the house, going late into the chamber where the maid-servants lay, saw no less than five of these lights together.   It happened a while after that, the chamber being newly plaistered, and a grate of coal fire therein kindled to hasten the drying of the plaister, that five maid-servants went to bed as they were wont, but it fell out too soon, for in the morning they were all dead, being suffocated in their sleep with the steam of the new tempered lime and coal.

Mrs Crowe, in her *Nightside of Nature*, tells a couple of stories which she heard from a 'dignitary of the Church,' born in Wales. A female relative of his started early in the morning, attended by her father's servant. When she had reached half way, where she expected to meet the servant of the friend she was about to visit, she dismissed the man who had accompanied her so far.   The fellow had not long left her before she saw a light approach her, moving about three feet above the soil.   She turned her horse out of the bridle-road, along which it advanced, to allow it to pass, but to her dismay, just as it came opposite her, it halted and remained flickering before her for about half an hour, and only vanished as she heard steps of the servant's horse, as he trotted up to meet and conduct her to her friend.   On reaching the house of her friend she related what she had seen.   A few days later that very servant who

had come to meet her sickened and died, and
his body was carried along the road upon
which the light had moved; and more curious
still, owing to an accident, the coffin halted
for an hour at the very spot where she had
been delayed confronting the mysterious
light.

That light, we may be sure, was supposed
to be the soul of a relative come from the
grave to meet and welcome a kinsman.   In
no other way can it be explained.

Another story is this :  A servant in the
family of Lady Davis, the aunt of the dignitary who told the above story to Mrs Crowe,
had occasion to start early for market.   Being
in the kitchen at 3 a.m., taking his breakfast, when every one else was in bed, he was
surprised by the sound of feet trampling down
the stairs; and opening the door, he saw a
light.   He was frightened and rushed out of
the house, and presently saw a gleam pass out
of the door and proceed towards the churchyard.   As Lady Davis was ill at the time, he
made no doubt that her death impended; and
when he returned from market his first question
was whether she were still alive; and though
he was informed she was better, he declared
his conviction that she would die, and described what he had seen and heard.   The

lady, however, recovered ; but within a
fortnight another member of the family died,
and her coffin was conveyed by bearers down
the stairs. One curious feature in the story
is that the man had described how he had
heard the sound of a bump against the clock
on the stairs; and actually, as the coffin
was being taken down, the bearers ran it
violently against the clock-case.

Mrs Crowe, in the *Night Side of Nature*, tells
a story narrated to her relative to Scotland,
showing that the idea of corpse-candles is not
confined to Wales. It was to this effect. A
minister, newly inducted into his cure, was
standing one evening leaning over the wall of
the churchyard, which adjoined the manse,
when he observed a light hovering over a
particular spot. Supposing it was some one
with a lantern, he opened the wicket and went
forward to ascertain who it might be; but
before he reached the spot the light moved
onwards, and he followed, but could see
nobody. It did not rise far above the ground,
but advanced rapidly across the road, entered
a wood, and ascended a hill till it at length
disappeared at the door of a farm-house.
Unable to comprehend of what nature this
light could be, the minister was deliberating
whether to make inquiries at the house or

return, when the light appeared again, accompanied by another, passed him, and going over the same ground, they both disappeared on the spot where he had first observed the phenomenon. He left a mark on the grave by which he might recognise it, and next day inquired of the sexton whose it was. The man said it belonged to a family that lived up the hill—indicating the house the light had stopped at—but that it was a considerable time since any one had been buried there. The minister was extremely surprised to learn, in the course of the day, that a child of that family had died of scarlet fever on the preceding evening.

Now, compare this story with that framed in the ballad of the *Little Blue Flame*, that contains a Devonshire tradition, and we find precisely the same phenomenon. A soul leaves the churchyard to fetch another of the family, and both appear as flames.

The poet Pfeffel of Colmar was blind, and he employed as his amanuensis a young Evangelical pastor. Pfeffel, when he walked out, was supported and led by this young man, whose name was Billing. As they walked in the garden, at some distance from the town, Pfeffel observed that whenever they passed over a particular spot, the arm of Billing

trembled and he betrayed uneasiness. On
being questioned, the young man confessed,
with some reluctance, that as often as he
passed over that spot, certain feelings attacked
him which he could not control, and that he
always experienced the same in treading in
a churchyard. He added that at night when
he came near such places he saw luminous
appearances. Pfeffel, with a view of curing
the youth of what he regarded as a fancy,
went that night with him to the garden. As
they approached the spot Billing perceived
a feeble light, and when still nearer he saw a
luminous ghost-like figure wavering over the
spot. This he described as a female form,
with one arm laid across the body, the other
hanging down, floating in an upright posture,
but tranquil, the feet only a handbreadth or
two above the soil. Pfeffel went alone, as the
young man declined to follow him, up to the
place where the figure was said to be, and
struck about in all directions with his stick,
besides running actually through the luminous
appearance; but the figure was not more
affected than a flame would have been. The
matter got talked about, and a great number
of people visited the spot; but it was not
till some months later that any investigation
was made. Then Pfeffel had the place dug

up. At a considerable depth was found a
firm layer of white lime of the length and
breadth of a grave, and of considerable
thickness. When this had been broken
through there were found the bones of a
human being. No tradition existed in the
place to explain this burial, whether it had
been a case of murder, or that the human being
here buried had died of pestilence, none could
tell—but it was abundantly clear that the
burial had taken place at some considerable
anterior period. The bones were removed,
the pit filled up, the lime scattered abroad,
and the surface again made smooth. When
Billing was now brought back to the spot,
the phenomenon did not return.

It is possible, it is even probable, that the
popular superstition relative to lights seen
above graves is due to the discharge of
phosphuretted hydrogen from a decaying
corpse. I drove over one day with my
brother to see a church, and before entering
it he thoughtlessly threw his overcoat across
a grave. On our return he fainted, being
overcome by the smell that his coat had
acquired. And this grave was not of recent
making, but was at the least eight years old.
It is possible enough that such exhalations
should become luminous, and thus start the

belief that is so general, and which has been expanded by imagination into the travelling of such lights to fetch others.

What, we may ask, is the Will-o'-the-wisp? Is it not the spirit of the man who has perished in a morass, dancing above where his body lies submerged? Some years ago a convict from Prince Town prison escaped. He was last seen flying over Foxtor Mire, and he never was seen again. Since then a blue flame has been observed occasionally hovering over the morass.

When the poet wrote :—

> Vital spark of heavenly flame,
> Quit, O quit, this mortal frame,

he uttered a sentiment expressive of the nature of the soul common to the many. None who have stood by a death-bed can fail to observe how closely the parting of soul and body, the light fading from the eyes, and warmth leaving the body, resembles the extinction of a fire.

In Yorkshire, when a man is drowned, in order to find the place where the body is, a lighted candle is stuck in a loaf of bread which is committed to the water, and the light after a while floats above the spot where the corpse lies below the surface. When I was in Yorkshire in 1865 a man was drowned in the Calder Canal, and this method was adopted before dragging for the body. In this case the candle-flame represents the soul going in quest of its husk.

In the legends of several of the Irish saints, the mother of one dreams that a spark has fallen into her mouth or her lap. It is the soul coming to her child. With this may be taken the Yorkshire notion of a falling star, already referred to.

Repeatedly in the Icelandic sagas one reads of the haug-eldir, cairn-fires, flames that flicker and wave above tumuli covering dead warriors who have been buried with their treasures. These fires are none other than the spirits of the dead guarding their plunder. The Esquimaux suppose the Northern Lights to be the spirits dancing about the Polar Circle.

There is at the present day, or was till recently, a morass near Stadr by Reykjanes in Iceland, where from the other side of the bay a wavering blue flame is seen, and it is supposed that a treasure lies sunken there ; but the light is that of the spirit of him whose gold lies beneath the marsh.

It was a belief among the German peasantry that the stars were human souls. When a child died its spirit was taken up to heaven and hung there as a star, but unbaptized children's souls became wills-o'-the-wisp. So also those of men who have moved their neighbours' landmarks. Above graves blue flames are seen to dance. Even unborn children are luminous, and this has been the occasion of many horrible murders of women expecting to become mothers, by men who desired to get hold of a hand of such an unborn, unbaptized child, by means of which they believed themselves able to send to sleep all in a house into which they entered for the purpose of robbery. We are distinctly told that it was the luminous character of the unborn that gave them this value.

A curious story is told in a letter from a German pastor in Elsass to the editor of *Magikon* (iv., p. 349). He had gone to Freiburg and was on his way home by night, and early in the morning, at 4 a.m., reached the first outlying houses of his village. The moon was in its last quarter, not a soul was stirring, when, in the road at about twenty or thirty paces from him, he saw a ball of fire burning in the middle of the way. The light given out was pale like that of spirits of wine. He halted and looked at it for some moments and then went forward, when the ball of fire rose with undiminished brightness

to the height of about twenty feet from the
ground and went to the graveyard, where it
descended again and vanished among the
graves. There was no trace of fire or ashes
on the highway where the fire had been first
seen. The pastor, whose name was J. I.
Schneider, wrote that he, along with his
children, had seen the same apparition a
second time.

But it is not only as a flame that the soul
is conceived to appear; it is supposed to
remain with the body. In the year 1882 my
grandfather renovated Lew Trenchard Church.
He swept away the rood-screen and the carved
oak benches and repewed the church. The
carpenter employed opened the vault of old
Madame Gould, the grandmother of my
grandfather. She had been a notable woman,
and he thought he would like to see her. It
was night, and he had his lantern. I tell the
tale as he told it me. When he opened her
coffin she sat up, and a light streamed from
her above that of his lantern. He was so
panic-stricken that he fled the church, and
ran home a distance of a quarter of a mile.
And as he told me, she followed him, and he
knew that, because his shadow went before
him the whole way. Arrived at his home, he
dashed in and jumped into the bed beside his

wife, who was ill, and *both* saw Madame standing before them, with a light shining about her, which gradually faded. He told me this story himself, with all the sincerity of a man who is speaking the truth. Next day he found his extinguished lantern where he had left it.

There are certain manifestations that may have helped on the popular superstition as to the soul being a fire, that may as well be mentioned. I cannot doubt myself that on occasions preceding death there is a luminosity apparent, as though the departing soul were shining through the body, as a candle does through the sides of the lantern. Sir H. Marsh, a London physician, writing in the *Medical Gazette* in 1842, gives an account of such an appearance that he had himself observed attentively.

But the soul has also been thought to take an animal shape. Guntram, the Frank king, was out hunting one day, as Paulus Diaconus tells us (iii. 34), when, feeling tired, he lay down under a tree to sleep. The squire, whilst guarding his royal master, with surprise saw a serpent emerge from the King's mouth and glide down to a rivulet hard by and seek to cross the water, but was unable to do so. Thereupon the squire, determined to see the end of the adventure, drew his sword and laid it over the stream from bank to bank. The serpent, seeing this improvised bridge, wriggled across and disappeared down a small hole at the foot of a hill on the opposite side. After remaining there for a while it returned along the sword and into the King's mouth. Soon after, Guntram, awakening, said that he had just had a most extraordinary dream, in which he thought that he had crossed a torrent on a bridge of steel, and entered a subterranean palace full of gold and jewels. The squire then relating what he had seen, Guntram set a number of men to work, the hill was undermined, and the treasure discovered. Thenceforth that hill bore the name of Mont-Trésor.

Helinand in his *Chronicle* tells a similar story. Henry, Archbishop of Rheims, and brother of King Louis, was travelling one summer with his retinue, and halted in the middle of the day for a rest. The Archbishop and some of his attendants went to sleep in the grass, but others kept awake, and these latter saw a little white animal like a weasel issue from the mouth of one of the sleepers and run down to a brook and try to cross it. Then the story goes on like that of Guntram, but without the discovery of treasure. When

the man awoke and was asked about what he
had dreamt, he said that he had been a long
journey and in it he had twice crossed a bridge
of steel.

Hugh Miller, in *My Schools and School-
masters*, when writing about a cousin named
George, says :—

He communicated to me a tradition illustrative
of the Celtic theory of dreaming, of which I have
since often thought.  Two young men had been
spending the early portion of a warm summer day
in exactly such a scene as that in which he communicated to me the anecdote.  There was an ancient
ruin beside them, separated, however, from the mossy
bank on which they sat by a slender runnel, across
which lay, immediately over a miniature cascade,
a few withered grass-stalks.  Overcome by the heat
of the day, one of the young men fell asleep; his
companion watched drowsily beside him, when all
at once the watcher was aroused to attention by
seeing a little, indistinct form, scarcely larger than
a humble-bee, issue from the mouth of the sleeping
man and, leaping upon the moss, move downwards
to the runnel, which it crossed along the withered
grass-stalks, and then disappeared amid the inter-
stices of the ruin.  Alarmed by what he saw, the
watcher hastily shook his companion by the shoulder,
and awoke him; though, with all his haste, the little
cloud-like creature, still more rapid in its movements,
issued from the interstice into which it had gone,
and flying across the runnel, instead of creeping
along the grass-stalks and over the sward, as before,
it re-entered the mouth of the sleeper just as he was
in the act of awakening.  'What is the matter with
you?' said the watcher, greatly alarmed; 'what
ails you?'  'Nothing ails me,' replied the other;

'but you have robbed me of a most delightful dream.
I dreamt that I was walking through a fine, rich
country, and came at length to the shores of a noble
river; and just where the clear water went thunder-
ing down a precipice there was a bridge all of silver,
which I crossed; and then, entering a noble palace
on the opposite side, I saw great heaps of gold and
jewels; and I was just going to load myself with
treasure when you rudely awoke me, and I lost all.'

I have little doubt that what Cousin
George saw was a humble-bee issuing from
the mouth of the sleeper, for this is the
form the soul is not infrequently supposed
to wear.[1]

These three stories are curious, as they
represent a premonition of the final departure
of the soul, which, according to a belief alluded
to by Sir Walter Scott, after departing from
the body has to pass over 'the brig of Dread,
no broader than a thread.' If it fall off it is
for ever lost; if, however, it attains the other
side of the gulf, it enters into the heavenly
palace.

My great-great-grandmother after departing
this life was rather a trouble in the place.
She appeared principally to drive back depre-
dators on the orchard or the corn-ricks. So
seven parsons were summoned to lay her
ghost. They met under an oak-tree that still

[1] In Lincolnshire a similar story is found, and there the
soul of the sleeping comrade did actually appear as a
bee.—*Notes and Queries*, ii. 506; iii. 206.

thrives. But one of them was drunk and forgot the proper words, and all they could do was to ban her into the form of a white owl. The owl used to sway like a pendulum in front of Lew House every night, till, in an evil hour, my brother shot her. Since then she has not been seen. But here again we have the Celtic idea of metempsychosis.

There is a ballad sung by the English peasantry that has been picked up by collectors in Kent, Somerset, and Devon. It is entitled *At the Setting of the Sun*, and begins thus :—

> Come all you young fellows that carry a gun,
> Beware of late shooting when daylight is done;
> For 'tis little you reckon what hazards you run,
> I shot my true love at the setting of the sun.
>> In a shower of rain, as my darling did hie
>> All under the bushes to keep herself dry,
>> With her head in her apron, I thought her
>> a swan,
>> And I shot my true love at the setting of the
>> sun.

In the Devonshire version of the story:—

> In the night the fair maid as a white swan appears;
> She says, O my true love, quick, dry up your
> tears,
> I freely forgive you, I have Paradise won;
> I was shot by my true love at the setting of the
> sun.

But in the Somerset version the young man is had up before the magistrates and tried for his life.

In six weeks' time, when the 'sizes came on,
Young Polly appeared in the form of a swan,
Crying, Jimmy, young Jimmy, young Jimmy is
    clear;
He never shall be hung for the shooting of his
    dear.

And he is, of course, acquitted.

The transformation of the damsel into a swan stalking into the Court and proclaiming the innocence of her lover is unquestionably the earlier form of the ballad; the Devonshire version is a later rationalising of the incident. Now, in neither form is the ballad very ancient; and in the passage of the girl's soul into a swan we can see how that among our peasantry to a late period the notion of transmigration has survived.

I was visiting an old woman who was bed-ridden, when one day she said to me: 'I saw my brother last night; he came flapping his wings against the window.' I stared, and asked for an explanation. Her brother had died some time previously. 'He came as a great black bird, like a rook but larger, and he kept beating against the glass. He is come to call me.' I endeavoured to give a natural explanation of the phenomenon, but she would not hear of that. She knew it was her brother by the tone of the voice. 'Beside, he warn't an over good man, and so he wouldn't

go into a white bird.  It was my brother and
no mistake.'

The Oxenham omen of the bird that
appears before a death in the family is another
instance, for the bird is probably supposed to
be the spirit reincarnate of an ancestor.

That the soul is on its travels when any
person is dreaming, or in a faint, or a cata-
leptic fit, is generally believed, and the various
revelations or visions of Heaven and Purga-
tory and Hell that have been given to the
world, from early times down to Dante's
*Divina Commedia*, derive therefrom.

A curious story was told by Mr John Hollo-
way, of the Bank of England, brother of the
engraver of that name.  He related how that
being one night in bed with his wife, and
unable to sleep, he had fixed his eyes and
thoughts with uncommon intensity on a
beautiful star that was shining in at the
window, when he suddenly found his spirit
released from his body and soaring into that
bright sphere.  But, seized with anxiety for
the anguish of his wife if she discovered his
body apparently dead beside her, he returned
and re-entered it with difficulty.

He described that returning as distressful,
like coming back to darkness; and that
whilst the spirit was free he was alternately

in the light or the dark, according as his thoughts were with the star or with his wife. After this experience, he said that he always avoided anything that could produce a repetition, the consequences of it being very distressing.

A citizen of Bremen had observed for some time that about the hour of midnight his wife ceased to breathe, and lay motionless like a corpse, with her mouth open. He had heard it said that souls could leave the body and go on their wanderings, and returned through the mouth. He could hardly believe it, but he resolved on trying the experiment on his wife; so he turned her body over when she was in this condition, with her face buried in the pillow. Then he went quietly to sleep, but on awaking next morning he found his wife in the position in which he had placed her, stone dead.

The conception of the soul passing into an animal form is distinctly Aryan. It is the basis of the Brahmin philosophy. The Celts, and after that the Teutons, brought with them from the East the belief in metempsychosis; but of this more in the next chapter.

## CHAPTER III

### THE BODY OF MAN

A FRIEND, a judge in Ceylon, had to sentence
a Cingalese to be hung for murder. The man,
when sentence had been pronounced, glared
at him and said : 'It is well, and shortly
after I shall be a dog and will bite and tear
you.' The doctrine of the Hindu as to the
spirit of man is that it passes at death into
some other body, presumedly that of an
animal. And that this was the belief of other
Aryan peoples can hardly be doubted. The
soul is immortal, imperishable, and it must
have a body into which to enter. Till it finds
such it hovers about uneasily.

Pythagoras and his followers taught that
after death men's souls passed into other
bodies, of this or that kind, according to the
manner of life they had led. If they had been
vicious, they were imprisoned in the bodies of
vile brutes, there to do penance for several
ages, at the expiration of which they returned
again to animate men; but if they lived
virtuously, some animal of a nobler kind, or
even a human creature, was to be their lot.

What led Pythagoras to this opinion was

the persuasion he had that the soul was of an
imperishable nature; whence he concluded
that it must remove into some other body
upon its abandoning this. That he derived
his doctrine from the Brahmins cannot be
doubted. It was a revolt against this belief
in an eternal revolution of existence that
led Buddha to start his scheme of escape
from it by making an opening for the soul to
free itself, by the destruction of passion, even
of all desire, so that the soul might reach
Nirvana, and be absorbed into the Godhead
whence it had emanated.

A few instances will suffice to show that the
transmigration of souls into animals was held
in Europe as well as in India.

In Luxembourg lived a gentleman who had
a daughter, his only child. An officer of the
garrison loved her, but as the father disapproved
of the match he sent the girl into a convent,
the windows of which were on the town wall.
The officer soon discovered where she was
and succeeded in opening communication with
her, and it was arranged between them that
she was to let herself down from her window
on the ensuing night at midnight. The
officer arranged with the soldier who was to
act sentinel that hour to lend his assistance.
However, such a hurricane of rain came on

that the commandant sent word round that the sentinels were to be changed every hour in place of every two hours. Thus it came to pass that a soldier was keeping guard under the wall who had not been initiated into the secret. At midnight, seeing something white descending, he shouted 'Who goes there?' and receiving no answer, fired and shot the girl. Since then every night a white rabbit is seen running along that portion of the fortification. It is the reincarnation of the girl.

At the beginning of the thirteenth century there lived a knight in the castle of Bierloz whose beautiful daughter was to be married to a young nobleman in the service of Duke Valeran of Luxembourg. The duke decided that the wedding should take place at Logne, where was his court. But when the damsel arrived there he himself fell in love with her, and on some excuse sent the young bridegroom-elect away, also the father, and his own duchess, and took the girl as his mistress, winning her heart by presents of jewellery and splendid clothes. The father died of grief, and the youth soon after fell. One night the girl had vanished and was sought for in vain. A day or two later a servant told his master that her corpse had been found at the entrance of a subterranean passage. The duke hurried to

the spot.  The body had vanished, but in
its place appeared a goat charged with glitter-
ing trinkets, that eluded all attempts to catch
it.  This mysterious goat is still visible.  Any
one who can catch it by the tail and hold
on will be drawn to where are collected the
precious articles received by the damsel.

In a good many places it is believed that
witches are transformed after death into
hares; and a lady wrote to me from the Isle
of Man that she could not get her servants
to eat hare, because it might be the body of
some old woman transformed.

It is not, however, only into quadrupeds
that human souls pass.  When I was a small
boy an old woman in the place, who could
neither read nor write, told me a folk-tale that
is very similar to one Grimm collected in
Germany.  A mother died, and the father
married again.  He had by his first wife a
daughter; by the second a son.  The brother
loved his half-sister dearly, but the wicked
stepmother hated her.  'Child,' said the stepmother one day, 'go to the grocer's shop and
buy me a pound of candles.'  She gave her
the money, and the little girl went, bought
the candles, and started on her return.  There
was a stile to cross.  She put down the candles
whilst she got over the stile; up came a dog

and ran away with them. She went back to
the grocer's and got a second bunch. She came
to the stile, set down the candles, and proceeded to climb over; up came the dog and
ran off with the candles. She went again to the
grocer's and procured a third bunch, and just
the same happened. Then she came to her
stepmother crying, for she had spent all the
money and had lost three bunches of candles.

The stepmother said, 'Come, lay thy head
on my lap that I may comb thy hair.' So
the little one laid her head in the woman's
lap, who proceeded to comb the yellow silken
hair. And when she combed, the hair fell
over her knees down to the ground. Then
the stepmother hated her more for the beauty
of her hair, so she said to her, 'I cannot part
thy hair on my knee, fetch me a billet of
wood.' So she fetched it. Then said the stepmother, 'I cannot part thy hair with a comb,
fetch me an axe.' So she fetched it.

'Now,' said the wicked woman, 'lay thy
head on the billet whilst I part thy hair.'
Well, she laid down her little golden head
without fear, and, whist! down came the
axe, and it was off. Then the woman took the
heart and liver of the little girl and she
stewed them and brought them into the house
for supper. The husband tasted them and said

that they had a strange flavour. She gave some to the little boy, but he would not eat. She tried to force him, but he refused, and ran out into the garden and took up his little sister, put her in a box, and buried the box under a rose tree; and every day he went to the tree and wept.

One day the rose tree flowered. It was spring, and there among the flowers was a white bird, and it sang sweetly. It flew to a cobbler's shop and perched on a tree hard by, and thus it sang :—

> My wicked mother slew me,
> My dear father ate me;
> My little brother whom I love
> Sits down below, and I sing above.

'Sing again that beautiful song,' asked the shoemaker. 'If you will give me first the little red shoes you are making.' The cobbler gave the shoes, the bird sang the song, and then flew to a tree in front of a watchmaker's, and sang the same strain.

'Oh, the beautiful song! Sing it again, sweet bird!' asked the watchmaker. 'If you will give me that gold watch and chain in your hand.' So the jeweller gave the watch and chain. The bird sang the song, and flew away with the shoes in one foot and the chain in the other, to where three millers were picking a millstone. The bird perched on a tree and sang the song, and as a reward for re-singing it had the millstone put round its neck as a collar. After that the bird flew to the house of the stepmother, and rattled the millstone against the eaves. Said the stepmother, 'It thunders.' Then the little boy ran out to hear the thunder, and down dropped the red shoes at his feet. Next out ran the father, and down fell the chain about his neck. Lastly, out ran the stepmother, and down fell the millstone on her head and she died.

This story must be older than the dispersion of the Aryan race, though, of course, it has undergone modifications. It is found among Greek folk-tales, also in Scotland as 'the milk-white doo,' also in Hungary, and in Southern France.

In *Faust* mad Gretchen in prison sings a snatch of this as a ballad.

I have given the tale at length, because it illustrates so fully what is the point now being insisted on. The bird is the transmigrated little girl. But that is not all. The dog that carries away the bunches of candles is the cruel stepmother who, in life, has transformed herself in this manner.

For as human souls after death go into the bodies of birds or beasts, so can they during life shift their quarters. This is the origin of the numerous tales of werewolves, and witches becoming cats or hares.

Among the Norsemen it was believed that witches could take even the shapes of seals— the only portion of them that they could not change was the eyes, and by them they might be recognised.

The word employed among the Norsemen for such as could change their shape was *eigi einhamr*, that is, 'not of one skin.' There were various ways in which they could change their shape. The original was that described in the Ynglinga Saga of Odin. 'He could change his appearance. There his body lay as sleeping or dead. But he became a bird or a beast, a fish or a serpent, and at a moment's notice could go into distant lands on his own business or on that of others.'

King Harold of Denmark required some information about the procedure in Iceland, and he induced a warlock to assume the shape of a whale and go thither. In the great battle in which Hrolf Krake fell in Denmark, one Bodvar Bjarki assumed the form and force of a bear, and fought furiously, whilst in the tent of the king his body lay as though dead. It was only when taunted because he appeared inactive that he rushed out into the midst of the fight in his human form, and fell.

A secondary stage was that in which one who was *eigi einhamr* threw over him a skin of a wolf or bear and then became that beast. The swan-maidens had their swan dresses that they laid aside to bathe. Velund stole one and thenceforth she was a woman. In like manner we have in Ireland and Cornwall stories of mermaids who laid aside their fish-like appendages—and these were seized by some onlooking peeping Tom, and he secured the damsel and made her his wife.

In the Völsunga Saga is a story of how King Völsung, who had married his daughter Signy to King Siggeir of Gothland, went on invitation to his son-in-law, along with his ten sons, and was treacherously waylaid and killed, with all his retinue except his sons. These were set in the stocks in a wood and left there to perish. The first night a huge gray she-wolf came, attacked, tore, and devoured one of the youths. Next night she came again and killed a second, and so on till only one was left, Sigmund. His sister Signy sent a trusty servant with a pot of honey, and instructions to smear with it the face of her one surviving brother, and to put some into his mouth. At night the she-wolf came, and snuffing the honey licked Sigmund's face and thrust her tongue into his mouth.

Thereupon he clenched his teeth on her tongue and a desperate struggle ensued.  The brute drove its feet against the stocks and broke them, but Sigmund tore out her tongue by the roots.  And that wolf was the mother of King Siggeir, who had assumed the vulpine form by her magic arts, and now perished miserably.

Many years ago, in fact in 1865, I published a *Book of Werewolves* that has long been out of print.  In it I collected all the stories I could find of transformation into wolves, and I have come across others since.  In fact it is apparently a universal belief that certain persons have the faculty of assuming a bestial form at pleasure.

Herodotos says: 'It seems that the Neuri are sorcerers, if one may believe the Scythians and the Greeks established in Scythia; for each Neurian changes himself, once in the year, into the form of a wolf, and he continues in that form for several days, after which he resumes his former state.'

Ovid tells the story, in his *Metamorphoses*, of Lycaon, King of Arcadia, who, entertaining Jupiter one day, set before him a hash of human flesh to prove his omniscience, whereupon the god transformed him into a wolf.

Pliny relates that on the festival of Jupiter, Lycæus, one of the family of Antæus, was selected by lot, and conducted to the brink of the Arcadian lake. He then hung his clothes on a tree and plunged into the water, whereupon he was transformed into a wolf. Nine years after, if he had not tasted human flesh, he was at liberty to swim back and resume his former shape, which had in the meantime become aged, as though he had worn it for nine years.

The following story is from Petronius :—

My master had gone to Capua to sell some old clothes. I seized the opportunity, and persuaded our guest to bear me company about five miles out of town; for he was a soldier, and as bold as death. We set out about cock-crow, and the moon shone bright as day, when, coming among some monuments, my man began to converse with the stars, whilst I jogged along singing and counting them. Presently I looked back after him, and saw him strip and lay his clothes by the side of the road. My heart was in my mouth in an instant; I stood like a corpse; when, in a crack, he was turned into a wolf. Don't think I'm joking: I would not tell you a lie for the finest fortune in the world.

But to continue : After he was turned into a wolf, he set up a howl and made straight for the woods. At first I did not know whether I was on my head or my heels; but at last going to take up his clothes, I found them turned into stone. The sweat streamed from me, and I never expected to get over it. Melissa began to wonder why I walked so late. 'Had you come a little sooner,' she said, 'you might at least have lent us a hand, for a wolf broke into the farm and has butchered all our cattle; but though he got off, it was no laughing matter for him, for a servant of ours ran him through with a pike.' Hearing this, I could not close an eye; but as soon as it was daylight I ran home like a pedlar that has been eased of his pack. Coming to the place where the clothes had been turned into stone, I saw nothing but a pool of blood; and when I got home, I found my soldier lying in bed, like an ox in a stall, and a surgeon dressing his neck. I saw at once that he was a fellow who could change his skin, and never after could I eat bread with him—no, not if you would have killed me.

Bodin tells some transformation stories, and professes that he had them on good authority. He says that the Royal Procurator-General Bourdin had assured him that he had shot a wolf, and that the arrow had stuck in the beast's thigh. A few hours after, the arrow was extracted from the thigh of a man lying wounded in bed. At Vernon, about the year 1566, the witches and warlocks gathered in great multitudes under the shape of cats. Four or five men were attacked in a lone place by a number of these beasts. The men stood their ground with pertinacity, succeeded in slaying one puss, and in wounding many others. Next day a number of wounded women were found in the town, and they gave the judge an accurate account of all the circumstances connected with their wounding.

Nynauld, who wrote a book on Lycanthropy

in 1618, relates how that in a village in
Switzerland, near Lucerne, a peasant was
attacked by a wolf whilst he was hewing
timber; he defended himself, and smote off
a foreleg of the beast. The moment that the
blood began to flow the wolf's form changed,
and he recognised a woman without her arm.
She was burnt alive. Any number of stories
might be instanced to show how widely spread
this superstition is, but these must suffice.
In the British Isles, whence wolves have long
ago been expelled, it is only hares and cats
that represent transformed witches.

There is, however, the old English romance
of *William and the Werewolf*, but this professes
to be a translation from the French. Gervase
of Tilbury, however, says in his *Otia Imperalia*:
'We have often seen in England, at changes
of the moon, men transformed into wolves,
which sort of human beings the French call
*gerulfos*, but the English call them *wer-wlf*;
*wer* in English signifies man, and *wlf* a wolf.'

In Devonshire transformed witches range
the moors in the shape of black dogs, and I
know a story of two such creatures appearing
in an inn and nightly drinking the cider, till
the publican shot a silver button over their
heads, when they were instantly transformed
into two ill-favoured old hags.

We now come to another form of transformation—a change of sex. I had an old carpenter many years ago who had been with my father before me, and he once told me that he knew of a man in Cornwall who had married, and became a father of a family; then he changed his sex, married, and bore a second family. Ovid tells the story of Iphis, a daughter of Ligdus and Telethusa of Crete. When Telethusa was pregnant her husband bade her destroy the child when born if it proved to be a girl, because his poverty was so great that he could not afford to rear a daughter. Telethusa was distressed, and the goddess Isis appeared to her in a dream and bade her preserve the child. Telethusa brought forth a daughter, which was given to a nurse and passed for a boy under the name of Iphis. Ligdus continued ignorant of the deceit, and when Iphis was full grown her father resolved to give her in marriage to Ianthe, the beautiful daughter of Telestes. A day to celebrate the nuptials was fixed, and mother and daughter were in consternation; but prayed to Isis, by whose advice the life of Iphis had been preserved. The goddess was favourable, and changed the sex of Iphis, and, on the morrow, the nuptials were consummated with the greatest rejoicings.

A better-known story is that of Tiresias, the Theban prophet, who as a boy was suddenly changed into a girl. Seven years after he again changed his sex, to his great satisfaction. Whilst he was a woman he had been married, and he was married again after he became a man.

Among the Icelanders it was believed that certain men became women every seventh day. That which caused the burning of the worthy Njall, his wife, and sons, in their house was the taunt of a certain Skarpedin, who threw a pair of breeches at one Flossi and bade him wear them, as he changed sex every ninth day. In the Gullathing laws is one condemning to outlawry any man who charged another with change of sex, or with having given birth to a child. When Thorvald the Wide-Travelled went round Iceland with a German missionary bishop named Frederick, preaching the Gospel, the smooth face and long petticoats of the prelate gave rise to bitter jests. A local poet sang a strain purporting that the bishop had become the mother of nine children of whom Thorvald was the father; and the Icelander was so furious that he hewed down the scald with his battle-axe.

We have seen now how that from the idea

or belief in metempsychosis possessed by the whole Aryan race, we have a series of superstitions relative to change after death into another animal form, and also changes, mainly voluntary and temporary, during life.

But there is still another class to which reference must now be made, and that is where the transformation is involuntary, the consequence of a spell being cast on an individual requiring him or her to become a beast or a monster with no escape except under conditions difficult of execution or of obtaining. To this category belong a number of so-called fairy tales, that actually are folk-tales. And these do not all pertain to Aryan peoples, for wherever magical arts are believed to be all-powerful, there one of its greatest achievements is the casting a spell so as to alter completely the appearance of the person on whom it is cast, so that this individual becomes an animal. One need only recall the story in the *Arabian Nights* of the Calenders and the three noble ladies of Bagdad, in which the wicked sisters are transformed into bitches that have to be thrashed every day.

But take such a tale as the *Frog Prince*. This is one of the most ancient and widely spread of folk-tales. It is found in the Sanskrit *Pantschatantra* (Benfey I. § 92), in

Campbell's *Tales of the Western Highlands* (No. xxxii.), in Grimms' *Kindermürchen*, No. I.; in Chambers's *Popular Rhymes of Scotland*, p. 52; in Halliwell's *English Popular Rhymes and Fireside Stories*, p. 48; and in numerous other collections. J. Leyden in his *Complaynt of Scotland* gives it. He says: 'According to the popular tale a lady is sent by her step-mother to draw water from the well of the world's end. She arrives at the well after encountering many dangers, but soon perceives that her adventures have not reached a conclusion. A frog emerges from the well, and, before it suffers her to draw water, obliges her to betroth herself to the monster, under the penalty of being torn to pieces. The lady returns safe; but at midnight the frog lover appears at the door and demands entrance according to promise, to the great consternation of the lady and her nurse.

> Open the door, my hinny, my heart;
> Open the door, mine ain wee thing;
> And mind the words that you and I spak
> Down in the meadow at the well-spring.

The frog is admitted and addresses her :—

> Take me up on your knee, my dearie,
> Take me up on your kneee, my dearie,
> And mind the words that you and I spak
> At the cauld well sae weary.

The frog is finally disenchanted and appears as a prince in his original form.

Here the story is told in its dryest and least poetical form. The prince had been bewitched into the form of a frog and could not recover his original shape till a girl had promised to be his wife, taken him into her chamber, and finally, in the English version of the tale, had cut off his head.

So in the Countess D'Aulnoy's story of *The White Cat*, the damsel has to cut off the cat's head before it can be transformed into a prince. In *Beauty and the Beast* we have much the same theme.

Professor Max Müller tried to establish that the story of the *Frog Prince* rose out of a misconception of the name of the sun in Sanskrit. But it has too many analogies for us to explain it thus. In the *Story of the Seven Ravens* the seven brothers of a damsel are bewitched into these forms till they obtain release through their sister. In an old Danish ballad a youth is transformed into a raven by a cruel stepmother, till his sister releases him by giving her child that he may pick out its eyes and drink its heart's blood before he can recover human form.

I was shown a cavern in the Vorarlberg where I was told that a hideous monster like

a gigantic toad had lived. It was a nobleman's son bewitched, and he could only be
released by a girl kissing him on the lips.
Several went to the cave, but were so repelled
by his unsightliness that they fled. One,
however, did remain and kiss him, whereupon
he recovered his human form and married her.

In the saga of Hrolf Kraki is an account of
King Hring of the Uplands in Norway, who
had a son named Björn by his wife. The
queen died, and Hring took a beautiful Finn
girl as his second wife. The king was often
away on piratical expeditions, and whilst he
was absent Björn and his stepmother had
constant quarrels. Björn had been brought
up with a well-to-do farmer's daughter named
Bera, and they loved one another dearly.
One day, after a sharp contest, the queen
struck Björn on the face with a wolf-skin
glove and said that he should become a rabid
bear, and devour his father's flocks.

After that Björn disappeared, and none knew
what had become of him; and men sought but
found him not. We must relate how that the king's
sheep were slaughtered, half a score at a time, and it
was all the work of a gray bear, both huge and grizzly.
One evening it chanced that the Carle's daughter
saw this savage bear coming towards her, looking
tenderly at her, and she recognised the eyes of
Björn, the king's son, so she made but a slight attempt
to escape; then the beast retreated, but she followed

it, till she same to a cave. Now when she entered
the cave there stood before her a man, who greeted
Bera, the Carle's daughter, and she recognised him,
for he was Björn, Hring's son. Overjoyed were
they to meet. So they were together in the cave
awhile, for she would not part from him when she
had the chance of being with him; but he said that
this was not proper that she should be there with
him, for by day he was a beast and by night a man.

Hring returned from his harrying, and was told
how this Björn, his son, had vanished, and also
how that a monstrous beast was up the country,
and was destroying his flocks. The queen urged the
king to have the bear slain.

One night as Bera and Björn were together, he
said to her : 'Methinks to-morrow will be the day
of my death, for they will hunt me down. But for
myself I care not; it is little pleasure to live with
this spell upon me, and my only comfort is that we
are together; and now our union must be broken.'
He spoke to her of many other things, till the bear's
form stole over him, and he went forth a bear. She
followed him, and saw a great body of hunters come
over the mountain ridges, and had a number of
dogs with them. The bear rushed away from the
cavern, but the dogs and the king's men came upon
him, and there ensued a desperate struggle. They
made a ring round him—he ranged about in it, but saw
no means of escape. So he turned to where the king
stood, and seized a man who stood next him, and
rent him asunder. Then was the bear so exhausted
that he cast himself down flat, and at once the men
rushed in upon him and slew him.

The king now went home, and Bera was in his
company. The queen now made a great feast, and
had the bear's flesh roasted for the banquet. The
queen came to Bera with a dish, quite unexpectedly,
and on it was bear's flesh, and she bade Bera eat it.
She would not do so. 'Here is a marvel,' said th
queen; 'you reject the offer which a queen herself

deigns to make to you.' So she bit before her, and the queen looked into her mouth; she saw that one little grain of the bite had gone down, but Bera spat out all the rest from her mouth, and said she would take no more though she were tortured and killed.

There are two points in this story deserving of notice. The one is recognition through the eyes, because it is through the eyes that the immortal soul looks out. The other is the effort made by the queen to get Bera to eat of the flesh, precisely as in the story of the *Rose Tree* the wicked stepmother endeavours to force the boy to eat the flesh of his sister.

In the story of Lycaon also lycanthropy was associated with cannibalism; and these tales seem to point back to a period when there was a revolt against such practice. Probably among the prehistoric natives conquered by the Aryans, cannibalism had been in vogue. St Jerome, speaking of the Attacotti in Britain, says that they were cannibals, and when a youth he had seen them.[1] At a low stage of development of civilisation, cannibalism was a recognised means whereby men acquired vigour, for by eating at least the heart or brain of a valiant enemy they thought that they assimilated to themselves his rare and valuable qualities. At a far later period Hrolf Kraki, finding a poor frightened

[1] Ipse adolocentulus in Gallia vidi Atticotos gentem Britannicum, humanis vesci carnibus.—*Adv. Ioviniun.*

boy who was bullied and beaten by the warriors in the king's hall, gave him to drink the blood of a brave warrior he had killed, and thenceforth this timorous youth became a mighty champion. In the story of Kulhwch in the old Welsh *Mabinogion* there is an account of how Gwyn 'killed Nwython, took out his heart, and forced Kyledr to eat his father's heart; thereupon Kyledr became wild and left the abodes of men.'

Even among the mediæval moss-troopers of the Scottish and Northumbrian border, there are instances both in history and tradition of their having eaten the flesh and drunk the blood of their enemies, and a certain Lord Soulis was boiled alive, and the murderers afterwards drank the broth made out of him.[1]

It is therefore not by any means improbable that the stories of forcing human flesh on those reluctant to eat it may carry us back to an early period when cannibalism was not done away with, but when the conscience had begun to revolt against the practice.

And who were these people who were cannibals? In the story of Björn and Bera the wicked stepmother was a Finn, and consequently not an Aryan. We are not told that the corresponding ill-disposed woman in the

[1] Durham Tracts (Folk-lore Soc.), I., p. 155.

story of the *Rose Tree* was of a strange race, but we are informed that the yellow hair of the little girl especially roused her dislike. And if she belonged to the dark-haired people who occupied the land before the Celts arrived, this is explicable.

That same people appear in household tales as giants. Not that they were actually such, but they acquired the reputation of being of extraordinary size because of the megalithic monuments they set up—giant's quoits, giant's needles, giant's tables, and the like. In the nursery tales they are credited with drinking blood and grinding men's bones to make their bread. The descendants of this race are still with us, and are not always on a level of intelligence with the fair-haired Englishmen who live hard by. That this primitive people believed in the transmigration of souls is not probable. Everything points to that doctrine having been the special property of the Aryans.

The Attacotti that Jerome saw, and who are mentioned by other writers as peculiarly ferocious men, were probably the lingering remains of the pre-Aryan inhabitants of the land; and the nursery tales about their devouring little children, and grinding men's bones to make their bread, are reminiscences of these fierce cannibal dolmen-builders.

## CHAPTER IV

### THE ANCIENT DIVINITIES

WE cannot expect to find reminiscences of the gods and goddesses of the primitive Silurian or Ivernian race that peopled Great Britain and Ireland, or even of the Celtic and Roman divinities, save in a most attenuated form. Even the saints of the Catholic Church who filled the religious horizon in England and Scotland for a thousand years have faded from it. But we will endeavour to discover some traces, and some do remain.

The prehistoric rude-stone building race certainly did have a goddess of Death, and probably one of Generation. In the subterranean excavations made in Le Petit Morin, by the Baron de Baye, the necropolises were guarded by rude figures representing a female cut in the chalk, and also by a representation of a stone hammer. The female figure has also been found cut on limestone in the department of Gard, on dolmens. In Brittany, in the covered alleys, there are numerous figures of stone axes or hammers, and also a curious shield-like representation that may possibly take the place of the female figure found in

F.-L.                                          E

the chalk tombs, but which it was difficult to
execute in granite.  On one of the slabs of a
dolmen, near Loudun, that I examined, was
cut a celt, and a celt is also cut on the huge
upper stone or table of the famous dolmen
of Confolens.  In Brittany, where the
incoming Celts from Wales and Cornwall
overflowed the land and submerged the earlier
peoples, these former have been largely
influenced by the people they treated as
belonging to a lower stratum of civilisation.

Here the cult of Death has acquired extraordinary importance, and M. Anatole le Braz,
a Breton folk-lorist, has written a treatise on
it, and collected the stories he has heard
relative to it.  In Léon Death may be said to
reign in undivided supremacy and tinctures
all existence, every amusement, every occupation.  La Mort is in Breton the *Ankou*, who
travels about the country in a cart picking up
souls.  At night a wain is heard coming along
the road with a creaking axle.  It halts at a
door, and that is the summons.  A spirit
passes, and the Ankou moves on.  Marillier,
who wrote a preface to M. le Braz's work,
says that Lower Brittany is before all else the
Land of the Dead.  'Souls do not remain
enclosed in the tombs, they wander at night
on the high-roads and in the lonely lanes.

They haunt the fields and the moors, thick as blades of grass or as grains of sand on the shore. They revisit their former habitations in the silence of the night, and from the *lis-clos* they can be observed crouched around the hearth, where the brands are expiring.' Certain mysterious rites are observed to which the curé is not invited, and where some old man is ministrant, on All Souls' even, on some granite-strewn height, about a fire. M. le Curé is discreet enough not to inquire too closely what goes on.

The wagon of the Ankou is like the death-coach that one hears of in Devon and in Wales. It is all black, with black horses drawing it, driven by a headless coachman. A black hound runs before it, and within sits a lady —in the neighbourhood of Okehampton and Tavistock she is supposed to be a certain Lady Howard, but she is assuredly an impersonification of Death, for the coach halts to pick up the spirits of the dying.

Now pray step in ! my lady saith;
  Now pray step in and ride.
I thank thee, I had rather walk
  Than gather to thy side.
The wheels go round without a sound
  Or tramp or turn of wheels.
As cloud at night, in pale moonlight,
  Along the carriage steals.

I'd rather walk a hundred miles
  And run by night and day,
Than have that carriage halt for me,
  And hear my lady say—
Now pray step in, and make no din,
  Step in with me to ride;
There's room, I trow, by me for you,
  And all the world beside.

Of course the notion of the death-coach is comparatively modern. It is an expansion of the ancient idea of Death coming to fetch the departing soul. Presumedly the earlier idea was of a bier. There is a remarkable account in Mrs Henry Wood's novel of *The Shadow of Ashlydiat* that gives us a notion of what the earlier superstition was. She is very emphatic over it that it is a real fact, and a fact of which she herself was witness.

Opposite to the ash trees on the estate of Ashlydiat there extended a waste plain, totally out of keeping with the high cultivation around. It looked like a piece of rude common. Bushes of furze, broom, and other stunted shrubs grew upon it. At the extremity, opposite to the ash trees, there arose a high archway, a bridge built of gray stones. Beyond the archway was a low round building, looking like an isolated wind-mill without sails.

Strange to say, the appellation of this waste piece of land, with its wild bushes, was the 'Dark Plain.' Why? The plain was not dark; it was not shrouded; it stood out, broad and open, in the full glare of sun-light. That certain dark tales had been handed down with the appellation is true; and these may have given rise to the name. Immediately before the archway, for some considerable space, the ground was entirely bare. Not a blade of grass, not a shrub grew on it—or, as the story went, *would* grow. It was on this spot that the appearance, the Shadow, would sometimes be seen. Whence the Shadow came, whether it was ghostly or earthly, whether those learned in science could account for it by Nature's laws, I am unable to say. If you ask me to explain it, I cannot. If you ask me, why then do I write about it, I can only answer, because I have sat and seen it. I have seen it with my own unprejudiced eyes; I have sat and watched it, in its strange stillness; I have looked about and around it—low down, high up—for some substance ever so infinitesimal that might cast its shade and enable me to account for it; and I have looked in vain. Had the moon been behind the archway, instead of behind me, that might have furnished a loophole of explanation.

No; there was nothing whatever, so far as human eyes—and I can tell you that keen ones and sceptical ones have looked at it—to cast the shade, or to account for it. There, as you sat and watched, stretched out the plain, in the moonlight, with its low, trunk-like bushes, its clear space of bare land, the archway rising beyond it. But on the spot of bare land, before the archway, would rise the Shadow, not looking as if it were a Shadow cast on the ground, but a palpable fact; as if a bier, with its two bending mourners, actually stood there in the substance. I say that I cannot explain it, or attempt to explain it; but I do say that there it is to be seen. Not often; sometimes not for years together. It is called the Shadow of Ashlydiat ; and superstition told that its appearance foreshadowed the approach of calamity, whether of death or of other evil, to the Godolphins. The greater the evil that was coming upon them, the plainer and more distinct would be the appearance of the Shadow. Rumour went that once, on the approach of some terrible misfortune, it had been seen for months and months before, whenever the moon was sufficiently bright.

I have quoted this at length, as it comes from Worcestershire, on the borders of Wales; and as it presents an earlier phase of the superstition than that of the death-coach.

There are stories in Henderson's *Northern Folk-lore* of coaches with headless horsemen, but I lay no stress on them, as these are evidently late developments of an ancient belief that Death, the Ankou, went about picking up souls as they departed.

To turn now to the celt or hammer figured on the graves of prehistoric peoples.

Both Strabo and Herodotus speak of peoples in Asia who, when their parents grew aged and useless, killed them. This was absolutely averse from the customs of the Aryans, who made the family and the clan a sacred centre. But it was quite possible with the non-Aryan natives before Britain was invaded by the Celts. Aubrey has preserved an account of how in churches hung behind the door 'the holy mawle,' with which sons might knock on the head their parents when they became effete and of no more use; and in a prose romance, Sir Percival congratulates himself that he is not in Wales, where sons pull their fathers out of bed and kill them. A Count Schalenberg rescued an old man who was being beaten to death by his sons, in Prussia, and a Countess Mansfield in the 14th century saved another in similar circumstances.

Now, this holy mawle, I take it, is no other than the celt or hammer that is figured on the dolmens and tombs of the prehistoric underlying population of Gaul and Britain. The Aryans would never have thought of putting their parents to death, though the parents might think it time to precipitate themselves down the *æternis stapi*[1] when provisions ran short. But that was a different matter. Suicide among the Norsemen was a self-sacrifice to Odin, and parent murder was never compulsory on the children.

Passing from the cult of the goddess of death, we come to that of the deity of life. I have at a rifle-shot from my own house a menhir, with a hollow cup in its top. The farmers were wont to drive their cows under it, and let the water from this cup dribble over their backs, under the impression that it would increase their yield of milk. My grandfather was so annoyed at this that he threw it down and buried it. I have dug it up and re-erected it, but the old superstition connected with it is dead.

[1] *Fornaldar Sögur*, iii. 7.

In Brittany are monoliths about which
women dance in a state of nudity, and rub
themselves against them in hopes of thereby
becoming mothers.  Near Dinan is the stone
of St Samson.  Girls slide down it, as it is on
an incline, and if they can reach the bottom
without a hitch, they believe that they will be
happy mothers when married.

Some of these stones are pitted with
artificially cut hollows.  The stones are
washed, to produce rain, are anointed, and
the cup-marks filled with butter and honey.
Most in France are now surmounted with
crucifixes, or have a niche cut in their faces
into which an image of the Virgin is inserted.
One in Brittany, at Tregastel, has carved on
it and painted a crucifix and the instruments
of the passion.  Such are all the deities that
we can safely say were culted by the prehistoric race that lies below the peoples that
successively overlaid them, of which any
trace remains in modern folk-lore.

We come next to Aryan folk-lore, and to
that in which there is some reminiscence of
the gods our ancestors once worshipped.  It
is remarkable that two common names for the
devil should enshrine those of ancient deities,
one Celtic and the other Teutonic or Norse.
These are 'The Deuce' and 'Old Nick.'

We learn from St Augustine that the Gauls believed in 'certain demons they called Duses,' and Isidore of Seville describes them as hairy. The word implies something higher than a mere satyr, for its equivalents are the Greek *Theos* and *Zeus*, the Latin *Deus*, the Sanskrit *Djous*, the Anglo-Saxon *Tiu*, from whom we get the name of the third day of the week, Tuesday. The corresponding god among the Germans was Zio, and among the Norsemen Tyr.

'As for the gods of the heathen they are but devils,' said the psalmist, and in this light did the Christian fathers and priests regard the gods. They were cast down from their thrones and treated as demons who had hitherto beguiled the heathen. Thus Tiu, or the Deuce, from being the god of the firmament and clear sky became a black devil, with the legs crooked as those of a goat.

There is a great cliff of granite rising precipitately above the River Plym that debouches at Plymouth, which goes by the name of the Dewerstone, or the rock of Tiu or of Tyr. On the top of this crag the Wild Huntsman is said to be frequently seen along with his fire-breathing Wish-hounds, and his horn is heard ringing afar over the moors, and as he chases the yelping of his hounds may be heard. He hunts human souls. Two old ladies who lived at Shaw, near by, assured me that they had often heard his horn and the yelping of the pack. A farmer was riding at night over Dartmoor when there came up alongside of him a mysterious hunter with his hounds running before him. The farmer, who had been drinking at the Saracen's Head Inn at Two Bridges, shouted, 'Had good luck—much sport? Give me a hare.' 'Take it,' replied the hunter, and flung something to the farmer, who caught and held it before him on the saddle. But it was too dark for him to see what had been cast him. Half an hour later he arrived at his house, and shouted for a servant to bring out a lantern and hold his horse. When a man arrived, 'Give me the lantern,' said he, 'and let me see what I have got.' He was obeyed, and the farmer raising the light saw on his other arm his own child dead. At the same moment it vanished. As in great consternation he was dismounting, the servant said to him : 'Sorry to have to tell you, farmer, but your poor little boy is dead.'

Children who die unbaptized join the hunt. Once two children were on a moor together; one slept, the other was awake. Suddenly the

Wild Hunt went by.  A voice called, 'Shall we
take it?'  The answer came, 'No, it will come
of itself shortly.'  Next day the sleeper was
dead.

Gervase of Tilbury says that in the thirteenth
century, by full moon towards evening, the
Wild Hunt was frequently seen in England,
traversing forest and down.  In the twelfth
century it was called in England the Harle-
thing.  It appeared in the reign of Henry II.,
and was witnessed by many.  At the head of
the troop rode the British king Herla.  He
had been at the marriage-feast of a dwarf in
a mountain.  As he left the bridal hall, the
host presented him with horses, hounds, and
horn; also with a bloodhound, which was set
on the saddle-bow before the King, and the
troop was bidden not to dismount till the dog
leaped down.  On returning to his palace, the
King learned that he had been absent two
hundred years, which had passed as one
night whilst he was in the mountains with the
dwarf.  Some of the retainers jumped off their
horses, and fell to dust, but the King and the
rest ride on till the bloodhound bounds from
the saddle, which will be at the Last Day.

Herla is, of course, the same as the German
Erl-King, and the name has gone into a
strange commutation as Harlequin, the

magician who performs wonders with his bat at Christmas.

Belief in the Wild Hunt is general throughout Northern Europe, alike among Celtic and Teutonic peoples, because what has originated the superstition is a simple natural fact that has been wrongly explained.  On the approach of winter flights of bean-geese come south from Scotland and the Isles, Iceland, and Scandinavia.  They choose dark nights for their migrations, and utter a loud and very peculiar cry.  A gentleman was riding alone near the Land's End on a still dark night, when the yelping cry broke out above his head so suddenly, and to all appearance so near, that he instinctively pulled up his horse as if to allow the pack to pass, the animal trembling violently at the unexpected sounds.

In Durham the Wild Hunt goes by the name of the Gabriel Hounds, and in Yorkshire it is the 'Gabble retchit.'  I cannot explain the derivation.  We may, I think, see in the wild huntsman either the Teutonic god Tiu or Tyr, or else the Celtic Duse.  'Old Nick' is none other than Woden, the chief god of our Anglo-Saxon forefathers, who has bequeathed to us the name of Wednesday,  He was also called Hnikare or Nikarr.  In Norway he has been degraded into a water-sprite or *Nix*.

Thor the Thunderer has left us his name in Thursday. According to Scandinavian belief he is red-bearded, and his hammer that he flings is the thunderbolt. A gentleman wrote to me in 1890 :—

It was in the autumn of 1857 or 1858 that I had taken some quinine to a lad who lived with his old grandmother. On my next visit the old dame scornfully refused another bottle, and said she 'knowed on a soight better cure for the ague than yon mucky stuff.' With that she took me round to the bottom of the bed and showed me three horse-shoes nailed there with a hammer placed crosswise upon them. On my expressing incredulity, she waxed wroth, and said : 'Naay, lad, it's a chawm. I tak's t' mell (hammer) i' moy left haun and I mashys they shoon throice, and Oi sez, sez Oi :—

Feyther, Son, an' Holi Ghoast,
Naale the divil to this poast !
Throice I stroikes with holy crook,
Won for God, an' won for Wod, an' won for Lok !

Theen, laad, whin the old un comes to shak him he wean't nivver git past you; you'ull fin' him saafe as t' church steaple.'

Could there be confusion worse confounded than this? The Holy Trinity invoked, and in the same breath God, Woden, and Loki—the very spirit of evil; and the Holy Crook and Thor's hammer treated as one and the same thing.

Yours faithfully,
B. M. HEANLEY.
Upton Grey Vicarage, Winchfield.

Clearly here God takes the place of Thor; and the Triad—Thor, Woden, and Loki—are equal with the Father, Son, and Holy Ghost.

Another interesting feature in this charm is that the ague is impersonated as an evil sprite, against whom the incantation is launched.

There is a shallow river, the Wulf, that runs through the parish of Broadwood Widger, in Devon. It discharges into the Thrustle, thence into the Lyd, and so into the Tamar. The Wulf is liable to sudden rises, and then becomes almost impassable, and was so till the County Council built a bridge. Previously one going to Broadwood, or leaving it to go east, was constrained to traverse a ford. Now it was believed, before the bridge was built, that there was a spirit of gigantic size who waited at the ford to carry foot-passengers over, and there is a woman still alive who insists that she was so conveyed across. That this belief owes something to a picture of a gigantic St Christopher that may have been in the church, but of which no traces now remain, is possible enough; that fresco, if it ever existed, did not, in my opinion, originate the conviction. The bearer across the stream is in all probability some ancient god, not happily in this case turned into a devil. Now I am convinced that this giant who wades through the river is none other than Thor, for in Norse story he is constantly represented as wading through the waters, above all the great river that flows round the terrestrial globe.  In the Younger Edda is the story of the battle between Thor and the giant Hrungnir. The latter fought with a stone club, which he flung at the Red-beard, who at the same moment cast his hammer.  The two missiles met in mid air and the club flew in pieces, one struck Thor on the head and sank in.  After Hrungnir had been killed, Thor went to visit the prophetess Groa, the wife of Œrvandil, to have the stone extracted.  She began her incantations, and Thor beginning to feel relief, in gratitude told her how that he had carried her husband over the River Elivagar, the great ice-stream that separates the realm of the giants from that of gods and men.  Œrvandil was conveyed across in a basket on his back whilst Thor waded across.  Unhappily one toe of Œrvandil protruded and got frost-bitten, whereupon Thor cut it off and threw it up into heaven where it became a star.  In the story of Hymir also Thor is represented as a wading god.  It is, therefore, not to be wondered at that St Christopher in Scandi-navian lands, Denmark, Norway, and Sweden, has stepped into the place and assumed the attributes of Thor.

Friday takes its name from Frî or Frija,

the goddess, the wife of Woden, the mother-goddess, as also goddess of tillage. She has been represented as holding a plough drawn by young children, as she gathers to her the spirits of those who die in infancy. To a certain extent she is the goddess of love, and so is equated with Venus, who has given her name to *Vendredi*.

Plough Monday is a festival of the past. It took place on the first Monday after the Epiphany, when a plough was decorated, and ploughmen were disguised and wore white smocks; there was a piper, and one dressed in fur with a fox's skin drawn over his head. The whole party was led by one Bessy, who went about collecting contributions. Bessy took the place of Frî, and the man in skins represented Woden, who was her husband. So much we may conjecture, but we have no certain evidence to establish this.

Frî or Frija appears however again and again as the White Lady. And here I will mention a circumstance that to my mind seems conclusive.

On 28th April, 1795, a young man whose relatives lived in this parish was returning home after having been some years in America. He hired a horse in Tavistock and rode to Lew Trenchard. It was a clear moonlight night, and as he rode through Lew valley, he looked into a newly ploughed field, in which a plough had been left. On this was seated a lady in white satin, with long hair floating over her shoulders. Her face was uplifted and her eyes directed towards the moon, so that he had a full view of it. He recognised her at once as Madame Gould, and taking off his hat called out, 'I wish you a very good-night, Madame.' She bowed in return and waved her hand. The man noticed the sparkle of her diamond rings as she did so. On reaching his home, after the first greetings and congratulations, he said to his relatives, 'What do you think? I have seen the strange Madame Gould sitting on a plough, this time of night, looking at the moon.'

All who heard it stared, and a blank expression passed over their countenances. 'Madame,' said they, 'was buried seven days ago in Lew Church.'

On that night, 28th April, the moon was seven days old and it set at 1.35 a.m. next day, approximately. Now the remarkable point in this story, which I heard from the family, is that Madame was seated on a plough; and the plough was the symbol of Frî.

For my own part, I believe that the

tradition of a White Lady was older than
Madame. It attached itself first to a certain
Susanna Gould, who was married in 1729 to
Peter, son of John Truscott, rector of Lew
Trenchard. Her father and the rector had
never been on good terms, and her father
resented the marriage. However, it took
place, and she died on her way back from
church, in her white wedding garments, and
was buried four days later.

Such a striking event naturally provoked
attention, and the earlier tradition of a White
Lady at once adhered to her, and clung to her
till some sixty-six years later, when it became
detached, and attached itself to another
notable lady of the same family.

I have troubled the reader with this story
only because I think the incident of sitting
on the plough is important as connecting the
White Lady of Lew Trenchard with Frî, the
Anglo-Saxon goddess.

To the north of us, but still in the parish,
is a deep and sombre valley, through which
gurgles a small stream. The road to Bratton
Clovelly descends into it; by the roadside was
a cave, that has now been blocked. It was a
common tradition that the White Lady was
wont to be seen by night beside the stream,
combing her long hair with a silver comb, and

scooping up water in the hollow of her hand, pouring it over her head, and it fell down in drops of pearl. The comb and the falling drops are all tokens that this White Lady was no other than Frî.

If I were to give all the stories of White Ladies that exist, I would fill a thick volume; but they all derive from the one source indicated. The White Lady, as in the case of the Hohenzollerns, is a death-token, because Frija is a death-goddess, to whom go the souls of the departed. A woman was once gathering sticks near one of the castles of the Hohenzollerns, named Schalksburg, when she missed her little son. After long search she found him and rebuked him for straying. 'Do not scold, mother,' said he; 'a beautiful lady in white took me on her arm, and she gave me this wild rose.' He showed his mother a pink dog-rose. She took the child home, and put the flower in water. After three days the rose withered, and with its withering the little boy was dead.

Saturday is the only day of the week that may take its name from a classic deity. In Italian it is *Sabbato*, *Samedi* in French, *Sabado* in Spanish and Portugese, *Samstag* in German, formed out of the Latin *Sabbatum*; and this is from the Hebrew describing the day as

one of rest.   But the last day of the week
among some Teutonic races has not been
named after the Sabbath, but after a heathen
deity.   In Westphalia it is *Saterdsas, Sâteres-
day* in Anglo-Saxon, *Saturdag* in the Nether-
lands.   Probably Saturn was taken as the
equivalent of the Norse God Sutur, the black
or seventh, not because evil, but as closing
the age of the world.   He seems to have left
no traces in folk-lore, unless that he be
identified with the Devil.   But 'Old Scratch'
is one of the names by which the Evil One
was designated, and which exactly agreed
with the popular imagination of the appearance of Satan when he chose to show himself.
For Skrati was the hairy wood faun of our
forefathers, and resembled the satyr of the
Romans, horned, and with legs like a goat's,
and the lower portion of the body covered
with hair.   The name is found not only in
English, Anglo-Saxon, Old German, and
Norse, but also among the Sclavonic peoples,
the Bohemians, the Poles, and the Slavonians.
Grimm could find no root for the name in
the German vocabulary; but in Slavonic,
*skrŷto* signifies to hide or keep in conceal-
ment, and this would well explain the
characteristic of the satyr hiding in the
woods and but rarely seen.

In an early version of the Psalms, in the place of the words 'from the pestilence that walketh in darkness,' in the 91st Psalm, we have 'from the Bug that walketh in darkness.' 'A Bug,' says Bayle, in his English Dictionary of 1755, is 'an immaginary monster to frighten children with.'

Each trembling leaf and whistling wind they hear,
As ghastly bug their hair on end doth rear,

wrote Spenser in the *Faerie Queene.* And Shakespeare uses the word several times. In *The Taming of the Shrew*: 'Tush! tush! fear (frighten) boys with bugs.' In *The Winter's Tale* : 'The bug, which you would frighten me with, I seek.'

'We have a horror for uncouth monsters,' wrote L'Estrange; 'but upon experience, all these bugs grow familiar and easy to us.' We use the word still in the form of Bogie and Bugbear and Bogart.

By its root we know that the word belongs to the same series of ideas as the Irish Phooka, the English Puck, the German Spük, and our modern word Spooke.

But whence came this form of the word? Sir Walter Scott, in *Harold the Dauntless*, makes Jutta, the outlaw's wife, by the Tyne, invoke Zernebock, by which is meant Tchernebog—the Black God, a Sclavonic deity.

In fact, God is Bog in the Sclave tongues.
Brelebog is the White God; but Grimm
greatly doubts whether among the ancient
Sclaves there existed any discrimination
between a White and a Black God.

As Zernebock does not satisfy Jutta by his
answer, she strikes the altar and exclaims :—

> Hence ! to the land of fog and waste,
> There fittest is thine influence placed,
> Thou powerless, sluggish Deity !
> And ne'er shall Briton bend the knee
> Again before so poor a God.

As a matter of fact, neither Briton nor
Northumbrian Scandinavian ever did bow
the knee to the Sclave Bog. The introduction of the Bug, Bogie, Bogart into our
Northern counties and into Scotland is due
to the extensive colonisation of all Northern
Britain by the Danes or Northmen. These
had been brought into contact previously
with Sclaves in Russia, where they founded
a dynasty, and along the Prussian and
Pomeranian shores of the Baltic; and they
had learned there to scoff at the Sclavonic God
and turn him into a bogie, much as later
Christian Anglo-Saxons converted the gods
of Valhalla into demons. The colonists
brought with them to Northumbria the conception of fiendish spirits as the gods of the

despised Sclaves.   We have no reason to
suppose that there ever was a migration of
Sclaves into Northumbria, bringing their
deities with them, and so giving rise to legends
of Bogies.   The Danish and Norwegian settlers
brought the conception ready-made with them.
The final degradation to which the supreme
deity of the Sclaves has had to submit
has been to confer a name on a particularly
offensive insect that does promenade in the
night and prove itself a torment.

# CHAPTER V

## SACRIFICE

In the year 1853, a farmer named J. S., in
Meavy Parish, between Tavistock and
Plymouth, a native of North Devon, lost
a good many cattle and sheep, due probably
to a change of pasture.   He accordingly took
a sheep to the top of Catesham Tor, killed
and then burnt it to propitiate the evil
influences which were destroying his flocks
and herds.   The offering had the desired
effect—he lost no more cattle after that.   He
told the vicar of the parish, the Rev. W. A. G.
Gray, at the time, or shortly after, and did

not seem to consider that he had done a superstitious thing.

Compare with this a communication made to Jacob Grimm, and inserted by him in his *Deutsche Mythologie*, p. 576, ed. 1843. It is a passage from a correspondent in Northamptonshire. 'Miss C—— and her cousin, walking, saw a fire in a field, and a crowd around it. They said, "What is the matter?" "Killing a calf." "What for?" "To stop the murrain." They went away as quickly as possible. On speaking to the clergyman, he made inquiries. The people did not like to talk of the affair, but it appeared that when there is a disease among the cows, or when the calves are born sickly, they sacrifice—that is, kill and burn one for good luck.'

In an adjoining parish to this, three years ago the churchwarden, a farmer, was troubled with murrain among his cattle, and he consulted a white witch, who bade him describe a circle on the ground with chalk in a field, obtain a white cock, and throw it up into the air, in the midst of the ring, when it would fall down dead, and the disorder would cease. He got a carpenter who works for me to throw up the cock. He did so, and the bird fell dead, as had been foretold. From that moment the cattle recovered. I was told this by the man who threw the cock, and he assured me that the bird actually fell dead.

In the Island of Mull, on the West Coast of Scotland, in the year 1767, there broke out a disease among the black cattle. Whereupon the people agreed to perform an incantation, though they were well aware it was not a very godly act. They carried a wheel and nine spindles of oakwood to the top of Carnmoor. Then they extinguished every fire in every house within sight of the hill. The wheel was then turned from east to west over the nine spindles long enough to produce fire by friction. If the fire were not produced before noon, the incantation lost its effect. They failed for several days running. This they attributed to the obstinacy of one householder, who would not allow his fires to be put out, as he did not approve of the proceedings. However, by bribing his servants, they contrived to have them extinguished, and on that morning kindled their fire. They then sacrificed a heifer, cutting it in pieces and burning the still warm diseased part. They then lighted their own hearths from the pyre, and ended by feasting on the remains. The words of incantation were repeated by an old man from Morven, who came over as master of the ceremonies, and who continued speaking all the time the fire was being raised. This man was living as a beggar at Ballocheog. When asked to repeat the spell, he declined, as he said that it was the act of this enchantment which had brought him to beggary, and that he dared not say the words again. The whole country believed him to be accursed.

Hunt, in his *Romances and Drolls of the West of England*, says, 'There can be no doubt that a belief prevailed until a very recent period, amongst the small farmers in the districts remote from towns in Cornwall, that a living sacrifice appeased the wrath of God. This sacrifice must be by fire, and I have heard it argued that the Bible gave them warranty for this belief.' He cites a well authenticated instance of such a sacrifice in 1800, and adds: 'While correcting these sheets I am informed of two recent instances of this superstition. One of them was the sacrifice of a calf by a farmer near Portreath, for the purpose of removing a disease which had long followed his horses and his cows. The other was the burning of a living lamb, to save, as the farmer said, "his flocks from spells which had been cast on 'em." '

Less than two centuries ago it was the

usage of a group of parishes which surrounded
Applecross, N.B., to sacrifice a bull on the
25th of August, the feast of St Thomas,
the patron saint; and the Presbytery of
Dingwall had frequent occasion to interfere
and interdict it. The sacrifice took place
usually in the island of St Rufus, or Innis
Maree, where the saint had a cell. From the
records of the Presbytery we learn that there
were monuments of idolatry in the island,
and stones which were consulted as to future
events; that the people adored wells and
poured libations of milk on hills.

To this day at King's Teignton, in South
Devon, a lamb is drawn about the parish
on Whitsun Monday decorated with boughs
and flowers, and contributions are solicited.
On Tuesday it is killed and roasted in the
middle of the village. The meat is then
sold in slices to any who will buy. The origin
of the custom is due to a remote period when
the village suffered from a dearth of water
and the inhabitants were advised to sacrifice
a lamb. They did so, and water sprang
up in an abundant fountain at Rydon, that
never fails even in the dryest summer. Since
then the lamb is sacrificed annually. Although
the custom has lost nearly all its Pagan
characters, yet it remains a survival.

Something very much the same took place every year on May-day at Holne, a village on the fringe of Dartmoor. But it has been discontinued of late years.

About 1869, in Moray, a herd of cattle was attacked with murrain, and one was sacrificed by burying alive.

Dr Mitchell says that in the North-west Highlands and Isles of Scotland, to cure epilepsy, a black cock must be buried alive, with a lock of the patient's hair and some parings of his nails. 'This is a cruel and barbarous thing, but is much more than that : it is a sacrifice deliberately and consciously offered in order to propitiate a supernatural power and effect the expulsion of the demon which is believed to have possession of the unfortunate epileptic. The ceremonies which attend the sacrifice leave little doubt as to its origin, or as to its past and present significance. It is nearly always gone about in a secret and solemn manner—in such a way as will just tend to secure its important object. A special superhuman agency, who is not the God of the Christians, is acknowledged and appealed to, and an effort is made to avert his malevolence. The whole idea and procedure are as truly heathenish as anything to be found among the savage nations of the world. Nor is this unfelt by those who practise the rite. They show their consciousness of it in a reluctance to tell of what they have done, and in the secrecy which they observe. This secrecy and this reluctance to speak freely testify also to the reality of their faith. . . . It would be a great mistake to suppose that the persons referred to are the grossly ignorant, and a still greater mistake to suppose that they are irreligious. On the contrary, they are often church-attending, sacrament-observing, and tolerably well-educated people—people, too, who necessarily participate in all the advantages of the advanced civilisation of their country.'[1]

We have seen that sacrifices are not completely done away with yet in Great Britain; and it is more than possible that a good number still take place without tidings of them reaching our ears.

We will now see what reminiscences yet remain of human sacrifices that took place in, not our land only, but on the Continent in remote days.

What is common in all such cases, as man becomes more civilised and humane, is to find a substitute for the human victim. We see that in the story of Abraham and Isaac,

[1] *The Past in the Present.* Edinb., 1889, p. 146.

when the patriarch was about to slay and burn his son, but found a substitute in the ram caught in a thicket by his horns.

Until his death, in 1884, William Pengelly, aged seventy-eight, was wont annually, at harvest thanksgivings, to bring a Cornman to the church, to be set up there as a decoration. It consisted of a small sheaf of wheat with the heads tied tightly together, and wreathed with flowers, and below, by means of a stick thrust through, two arms were found, and five stalks of barley were bound about each protruding portion of the stick, with the heads standing out to represent fingers. Before harvest thanksgivings were instituted, the Cornman was taken to the barn and there suspended.

It was not invariable that the arms should be formed, and I have seen the Cornman without them, or with only indications of arms. As such, if I do not mistake, he is represented as many as eight times on the carved oak benches of Altarnon Church in Cornwall.

Mr Hunt, in his *Romances and Drolls of the West of England*, thus describes what used to be called 'Crying a neck' at harvest.

'After the wheat is all cut on most farms in Cornwall and Devon, the harvest people

have a custom of "crying a neck." I believe
that this practice is seldom omitted on any
large farm in these counties. It is done in
this way. An old man, or some one else
well acquainted with the ceremonies used on
the occasion, when the labourers are reaping
the last field of wheat, goes round to the
shocks of sheaves and picks out a little
bundle of all the best ears he can find; this
bundle he ties up very neat and trim, and
plaits and arranges the straws very taste-
fully. This is called "the neck" of wheat,
or wheaten-ears. After the field is cut out
and the pitchers once more circulated, the
reapers, binders, and the women stand round
in a circle. The person with "the neck"
stands in the centre, grasping it with both
his hands. He first stoops and holds it near
the ground, and all the men forming the ring
take off their hats, stooping and holding them
with both hands towards the ground. They
then all begin at once, in a very prolonged
and harmonious tone, to cry, "The Neck."
At the same time slowly raising themselves
upright and elevating their arms and hats
above their heads, the person with "the neck"
also raising it on high. This is done three
times. They then change their cry to "We
yen! We yen!" which they sound in the

same prolonged and slow manner as before, with singular harmony and effect, three times. The last cry is accompanied by the same movements of the body and arms as in crying "The Neck." After this they all burst out into a kind of loud joyous laugh, flinging up their hats and caps into the air, capering about, and perhaps kissing the girls. One of them then gets "the neck" and runs as hard as he can down to the farm-house, where the dairymaid, or one of the young female domestics, stands at the door prepared with a pail of water. If he who holds "the neck" can manage to get into the house in any way unseen, or openly by any other way than the door at which the girl stands with the pail of water, then he may lawfully kiss her; but, if otherwise, he is regularly soused with the contents of the bucket. "The neck" is generally hung up in the farm-house, where it often remains for three or four years.'

Mr Hunt wrote in 1865. Since then the custom has almost if not wholly ceased to be observed, owing to the general abandonment of the sickle and the introduction of reaping machines.

Mr Hunt is wrong in supposing that 'We yen' is a corruption of 'We have done,' it is 'We hae 'im!' *i.e.* we have taken the corn spirit. I, in my boyhood, often saw 'the neck' crying. Mrs Bray, in a letter to Robert Southey, 1832, gives a description of 'Cutting the neck,' but she missed the final ceremony : the flight of the man who carries it and gets drenched with water. 'We were passing near a field on the fringe of Dartmoor, where the reapers were assembled. In a moment the pony started nearly from one side of the way to the other, so sudden came a shout from the field which gave him this alarm. On my stopping to ask my servant what all this noise was about, he seemed surprised by the question, and said, "It was only the people making their games, as they always did, to the spirit of the harvest." ' She then goes on to describe the ceremony much in the same way as Mr Hunt, only that, according to her, the reapers hold their sickles aloft, not their hats, and as I remember it, her account is correct. She also gives the cry as 'Wehaven! Wehaven!'

The meaning of this usage would quite escape us unless we had analogous customs elsewhere to elucidate it. The whole matter has been gone into with great minuteness by Sir J. Fraser in *The Golden Bough*, and therefore I will not enter into it here fully, but

give a summary of facts connected with it.
But prior to doing so, I will quote two accounts
of similar usages in Bavaria from Ganghofer's
*Oberland*, 1884. The girl who is last in the
driving out of the sheep is mocked by the
youths, who make a man of straw and nail
it up against the stall door. The girl seeks to
defend herself with a bucket of water, but
the youths also bring pails of water, and in
the end all get thoroughly drenched. This
takes place at Tegernsee on Whitsun Monday.

Elsewhere in Bavaria is performed the
Santrigel ceremony. A boy or young man,
on Whitsunday, is wrapped up in green
boughs from head to foot, is seated on the
leanest cow of the village, with a band going
before him, and he is conveyed to the edge
of a lake or river and is there thrown in.
As on more than one occasion a Santrigel
narrowly escaped drowning, the authorities
forbade this; and the flinging into the river
or lake is commuted into sousing with a bucket
of water.

Both these examples represent a sacrifice
to the goddess of the Spring, in which either
a lad or a girl was ceremonially drowned.
And in the Cornish example of the Neck,
the lad flying with the cornman and met by
a pail of water thrown over him, leads us

to trace back to a time when he was actually drowned. These Bavarian examples concern spring customs, but harvest customs resemble them closely. In some parts of Europe the corn spirit is regarded as female, and is spoken of as the corn mother; and in such cases it is a woman who makes up the figure out of corn straw, or else is wrapped up in straw and led about processionally. The cutting of the last shock is supposed to be the killing of the corn spirit. Sometimes, and that not infrequently, a youth or a woman is wrapped up in the straw and treated very roughly—only now not slain. In a good many cases the corn man or woman was not drowned but burnt.

Owing to the distress caused in a small community by the sacrifice by water or fire of one of its members, it became customary to seize on a stranger passing by, or entering the cornfield. He was constrained to ransom himself by a payment. Thus, in Essex, if one not a reaper ventures into a cornfield, the workmen rush upon him, surround him, shouting 'A largess! a largess!' and beat him very unhandsomely unless he pays to escape.

In Phrygia we are told that Lityertes, son of King Midas, used to reap the corn; but when a stranger chanced to enter the field

he forced him to reap along with himself.
Finally he would wrap the stranger in a sheaf,
cut off his head with a sickle, and carry away
his body wrapt in the straw. But at last he
was himself slain by Hercules, who threw
his body into the river. As Hercules was
probably reported to have slain Lityertes in
the same way in which Lityertes slew others,
we may infer that Lityertes was wont to
throw the bodies of his victims into the river.

Sir J. Fraser says that there is ground for
supposing that in such a story ' we have the
description of a Phrygian harvest custom in
accordance with which certain persons, especially strangers, passing the harvest-field, were
regularly regarded as embodiments of the
corn spirit, and as such were seized by the
reapers, wrapt in sheaves, and beheaded; their
bodies, bound up in the cornstalks, being
afterwards thrown into water as a rain-charm.
The grounds for this supposition are—first,
the resemblance of the Lityertes story to the
harvest customs of European peasantry; and
second, the fact that human beings have been
commonly killed by savage races to promote
the fertility of the fields.'

Sir J. Fraser, following Mannhardt, produces
an enormous number of instances, far too
many to be given here.

Savage races at the present day sacrifice
human beings for the prosperity of their
harvest. At Lagos in Guinea it was the custom
annually to impale a young girl alive soon
after the spring equinox, in order to secure
good crops. The Marinos, a Bechuana tribe,
sacrifice a human being for the same purpose,
and choose as stout a victim as they can find.
He is killed among the wheat, and his blood
is burned along with the frontal bone, the
flesh, and brain, and the ashes are dispersed
over the fields to fertilise the soil.

The Gonds of India were wont to kidnap
Brahmin boys; at sowing and reaping,
after a triumphal procession, one of them was
sacrificed, his blood was sprinkled over the
ploughed field or the ripe crops, and his flesh
was devoured.

The Khonds are a native race in Bengal.
What we know of them is from accounts by
British officers engaged in putting them
down some sixty years ago. They regularly
sacrificed to ensure good crops. The victim
or Meriah must be purchased, or be the son
of a victim. Khonds often sold their children
for the purpose, 'considering the beatification
of their souls certain, and their death, for the
benefit of mankind, the most honourable
possible.' A victim was always treated with

great respect as one consecrated to the
earth goddess.

A Meriah youth, on attaining maturity,
was given a wife, who was herself fore-
doomed to be sacrificed. Their offspring
were also victims. The periodical sacrifices
were generally so arranged that every head
of a family was enabled, at least once a year,
to procure a shred of flesh for his fields.

The mode of procedure was as follows :—
Ten or twelve days before the sacrifice the
victim had his hair cut. Crowds of men and
women assembled to witness the sacrifice.
None might be excluded, since it was for the
benefit of all. The victim, dressed in a new
garment, was led processionally from the
village with music and dancing, to a sacred
grove, where the Meriah, anointed and crowned
with flowers, was tied to a post. That the
victim might not resist, his arm-bones were
broken, or else he was drugged with opium.
Then he was strangled, squeezed to death, or
cut up alive, the crowd rushing upon him
to hack the flesh from his body with their
knives and carry strips away to bury in their
fields.

In one district the victim was put to death
slowly by fire. A low stage was formed,
sloping on each side like a roof; upon it the

victim was placed, his limbs wound round with cords to confine his struggles. Fires were then lighted and hot brands applied to make him roll up and down the slopes of the stage as much as possible, for the more tears he shed the more abundant would be the supply of rain. When these sacrifices were put down by the British Government, goats, etc., were substituted for human victims.

Now those who perpetrated these horrors were not the Aryan Hindus, but the Dravidian races underlying them; and there is reason to suppose that similar sacrifices that took place in Europe pertained to the religious rites of the population that formed the bed-rock over which were formed the various strata by invasion of Celt and Teuton. With the exception of the Khonds, no deity was recognised, and those who reported these sacrifices may not have understood that the cult was to spirits and not to gods and goddesses.

Sir James Fraser gives four reasons for thus considering them :—

'1. No special class of persons is set apart for the performance of the rites; in other words, there are no priests. The rites may be performed by any one as occasion demands.

'2. No special places are set apart for the

performance of the rites; in other words, there are no temples. The rites may be performed anywhere as occasion demands.

'3. Spirits, not gods, are recognised.

'4. The rites are magical rather than propitiatory. In other words, the desired objects are attained, not by propitiating divine beings by sacrifice, but by ceremonies which are believed to influence the course or nature directly through a physical sympathy or resemblance between the rite and the effect which it is the intention of the rite to produce.'[1]

We will pass now to another point, the selection of the victim to be sacrificed; and here we have preserved traces of the process, and that in children's counting-out games.

Tacitus tells us that the ancient Germans were wont to determine matters of importance by lot. They broke off twigs of a green tree, cut them into equal lengths and put on them signs distinguishing one from another. These were cast at random upon a white cloth, and the priest of the tribe or the house father drew a lot, and guidance as from heaven was supposed to be thus given. The use of lots continued in vogue among the Saxons till a late period, in spite of the efforts of the clergy,

---

[1] *The Golden Bough.* 1890, I., p. 348.

who sought to limit application to lot to
the cases where human judgment could
not be certain of being right. It was still
current in Germany in the seventh century,
and with less change of adjuncts than we
usually find in the adoption of heathen forms
even by Christian saints.

That the lot was used to determine a sacrifice we know from the story of Jonah. When
the storm fell on the ship the sailors 'said
every one to his fellow, Come, and let us
cast lots, that we may know for whose cause
this evil is upon us. So they cast lots,
and the lot fell upon Jonah.'

In very much—indeed in exactly the same
way—it is determined who is to be thrown
overboard, in an old English ballad still sung
by our peasantry :—

'Twas of a sea-captain came o'er the salt billow,
He courted a maiden, down by the green willow.
'O take of your father his gold and his treasure !
O take of your mother her fee without measure.'

The damsel robs her parents, and flies with
the sea captain in his vessel.

And when she had sailed to-day and to-morrow,
She was wringing her hands, she was crying in
sorrow.
And when she had sailed, the days were not many,
The sails were outspread, but of miles made not
any.

> They cast the black bullets as they sailed on the
>     water;
> The black bullet fell on the undutiful daughter.
> Now who in the ship must go over the side, O !
> O none save the maiden, the fair captain's bride, O !

So the undutiful daughter is thrown overboard.

Tylor, in his *Primitive Culture*, holds that
things held of highest importance and greatest
weight by men in a savage state become the
playthings of children in a period of civilisation; thus the bow and arrow, once the only
means men had of obtaining food in the chase,
and a main means of defence and assault in
war, have become toys in the hands of civilised
children at the present day.    Adopting this
theory, we may see how that methods of
determining life or death in ancient times may
now have degenerated into children's games.

The casting of lots was used by savage
tribes as a means of selecting from a company
of slaves or prisoners the unhappy individual
who was to be offered in sacrifice; and one
form of selection was by counting-out rhymes.

In an essay on *Wandering Words* Mr
T. W. Sandrey says :—'The talismanic words
uttered by children in their innocent games
have come down to us very nearly as perfect
as when spoken by the ancient Briton, but
with an opposite and widely different meaning.

The only degree of likeness that lies between them now is, that where the child of the present day escapes a certain kind of juvenile punishment, the retention of the word originally meant DEATH in its most cruel and barbarous way.' The correspondence, as Mr H. C. Rothes has pointed out, is much closer than the writer perceived, for he overlooked the fact that the process in both instances is one of elimination, the one remaining being the victim, the rest being successively set free.

I have tried in my novel *Perpetua*[1] to give a description of what took place, according to tradition, at Nîmes once in every seven years. Nîmes possesses a marvellous spring, a river of green water that swells up out of the bowels of the earth and fills a large circular reservoir. A temple of Nemausus stood near the basin, and Nemausus was the tutelary god of the town.

'On the 1st of March, in the year 218, the inhabitants of the town were congregated near the fountain, all in holiday costume. Among them ran and laughed numerous young girls, all with wreaths of white hyacinths or of narcissus on their heads. Yet, jocund as the scene was, to such as

---

[1] *Perpetua*. Lond.: Isbister & Co. 1897.

looked closer there was observable an under-current of alarm that found expression in the faces of the older men and women of the throng, at least in those of such persons as had their daughters flower-crowned.

'For this day was especially dedicated to the founder and patron of the town, who supplied it with water from his unfailing urn, and once in every seven years a human victim was offered in sacrifice to the god Nemausus, to ensure the continuance of his favour by a constant efflux of water, pure, cool, and salubrious.

'The victim was chosen from among the daughters of the old Gaulish families of the town, and was selected from among girls between the ages of seven and seventeen. None knew which would be chosen and which rejected. The selection was not made by either priest or priestess attached to the temple. Nor was it made by the magistrates. Chance or destiny alone determined who was to be chosen out of the forty-nine who appeared before the god.

'When the priests and priestesses drew up in lines between the people and the fountain, the ædile of the city standing forth, read out from a roll the names of seven times seven maidens; and as each name was called, a white-robed flower-crowned child fluttered from among the crowd and was received by the priestly band.

'When all forty-nine were gathered together, they were formed into a ring, holding hands, and round this ring passed the bearers of the silver image of the god. As they did so, suddenly a golden apple held by the god fell and touched a graceful girl who stood in the ring.

' "Come forth, Lucilla," said the chief priestess. "Speak thou the words. Begin."

'Then the damsel loosed her hands from those she held, stepped into the midst of the circle, and raised the golden pippin. At once the entire ring of children began to revolve like a dance of white butterflies in early spring; and as they swung from right to left, the girl began to recite at a rapid pace a jingle of words in a Gallic dialect that ran thus :—

> One and two,
> Drops of dew.
> Three and four,
> Shut the door.

As she spoke she indicated a child at each numeral—

> Five and six,
> Pick up sticks;
> Seven and eight,
> Thou must wait.

Now passed a thrill through the crowd. The children whirled quicker.

> Nine and ten,
> Pass again.
> Golden pippen, lo ! I cast
> Thou, Alemene, touched at last.

'At the word '' last,'' she threw the apple, struck a girl, and at once left the ring, cast her coronet of narcissus into the fountain, and ran into the crowd. For her the risk was past, as she would be over age when the next septennial sacrifice came round.

'Now it was the turn of Alcmene. She held the ball, paused a moment, looking about her, and then, as the troop of children revolved she rattled the rhyme and threw the pippin at a damsel named Tertiola. Whereupon she, in her turn, cast her garland of white violets and withdrew.

'Again the wreath of children circled, and Tertiola repeated the jingle till she came to "Touched at last," when ʌ girl named Ælia was selected and came into the middle. This was a child of seven, who was shy and clung to her mother. "My Ælia ! Rejoice that thou art not the victim. Be speedy with the verse, and I will join the *crustula*."

'So encouraged, the frightened child rattled out some lines, then halted, her memory had

failed, and she had to be reminded of the rest.
At last she also was free, ran to her mother's
bosom, and was comforted with cakes.

'Now arrived the supreme moment—that
of the final selection.  The choosing girl, in
whose hand was the apple, stood before those
who alone remained.  She began :—

> One, two,
> Drops of dew.

Although there was so vast a concourse
present, not a sound could be heard save the
voice of the girl repeating the jingle, and the
rush of the holy water over the weir.  Every
breath was held.

> Nine and ten,
> Pass again.
> Golden pippin, now I cast
> Thou, Portumna, touched at last.

At once the girl who had cast the apple withdrew, so also did the girl who skipped to the
basin and cast in her garland.  One alone
remained—Perpetua; and the high priestess,
raising her hand, stepped forward, pointed
to her, and said "Est." '

I have ventured to reproduce this, which,
although fiction, undoubtedly represents what
actually took place.

I will now quote Mr Bolton in *Counting-
out Rhymes* :—

'Children playing out-of-door games, such

as Hide-and-seek and "I spy," in which one
of their number has to take an undesirable
part, adopt a method of determining who
shall bear the burden which involves the
principle of casting lots, but differs in manner
of execution.  The process in Scotland is
called "clapping out" and "fitting out";
in England it is commonly known as "counting out."   It is usually conducted as follows :—
A leader, generally self-appointed, having
secured the attention of the boys and girls
about to join in the proposed game arranges
them in a row, or in a circle about him as fancy
may dictate.   He (or she) then repeats
a peculiar doggerel, sometimes with a rapidity
which can only be acquired by great familiarity
and a dexterous tongue, and pointing with the
hand or forefinger to each child in succession,
not forgetting himself (or herself), allots to
each one word of the mysterious formula :—

> One-ery, two-ery, ickery, Ann,
> Filling, falling, Nicholas, John;
> Que-ever, quaver, English, knaver,
> Stinhilum, Stanhilum, Jericho, buck.

This example contains sixteen words.   If
there be a greater number of children a
longer verse is used ; but generally the number
of words is greater than the number of
children, so that the leader begins the round

of the group a second time, giving to each child one word of the doggerel. Having completed the verse or sentence, the child on whom the last word falls is said to be "out," and steps aside.

'After the child thus counted out has withdrawn, the leader repeats the same doggerel with the same formalities, and, as before, the boy or the girl to whom the last word is allotted stands aside—is "out." The unmeaning doggerel is repeated again and again to a diminishing number of children, and the process of elimination is continued until only two of them remain. The leader then counts out once more, and the child not set free by the magic word is declared to be "IT," and must take the objectionable part in the game.

'The word *IT* is always used in this technical sense, denoting the one bearing the disagreeable duty; no child questions its meaning, nor have we learned of any substitute for this significant monosyllable. The declaration of a child, "You are *It* !" following the process of counting out, seems to carry with it the force of a military order, and is in many cases more promptly obeyed than a parent's command.'[1]

[1] H. C. Bolton. *The Counting-out Rhymes of Children*. Lond., 1888, pp. 1–2.

I pass now to an entirely different phase of folk-lore, but still connected with sacrifice.

It is said in Devonshire that the river Dart every year claimeth a heart. That is to say, that this river demands a human offering. At Huccaby Bridge is heard, in certain conditions of the wind the 'Cry of the Dart,' a strange wailing and then shrieking call. And it is supposed that this is the demand of the river for a victim. Some few years ago there was a marriage at Staverton church of a couple, one from Dartington. The party crossed the river at a ford in a cart. On their return there ensued a sudden freshet, and the conveyance was swept away and all drowned. 'It is only the Dart demanding her hearts,' was the comment on this occasion.

Sir Walter Scott, in *The Pirate*, notices the repugnance felt in rescuing drowning men from a wreck. The feeling is that the Sea, or the Goddess of the Sea, demands her victims. Among the seamen of Orkney and Shetland it was formerly deemed unlucky to rescue persons from drowning, since it was held as a matter of religious faith that the sea is entitled to certain victims, and if deprived would avenge itself on those who interfere.

On the Cornish coast the sea is heard calling for its victim. A fisherman or a pilot walking

one night on the sands at Porth-Towan, whe
all was still save the monotonous fall of tl.
light waves upon the sand, distinctly hear
a voice from the sea exclaiming,—

The hour is come, but not the man.

This was repeated three times, when :
black figure, like that of a man, appeared on
the top of the hill. It paused for a moment,
then rushed impetuously down the stee
incline, over the sands, and was lost in th
sea.

Mr Hunt says that this story is told in
different forms all round the Cornish coast.

In Whydah, Africa, the king sends a young
man annually to be thrown into the sea.
In the Issefjord, a part of the Cattegat Strait.
a sea-demon formerly dwelt who stopped
every ship and demanded a man from it.
But the priests exorcised it by exposing
the head of St Lucius, the pope.

When Xerxes, in the course of his conquests,
came to the sea, he sacrificed a human lif
to the Hellespont; and at Artemisium th
handsomest Greek captive was slain over th
bows of the admiral's ship.

Saxo Grammaticus tells how a Norseman's
ship was mysteriously stopped at sea until
a man was thrown overboard. Kinloch says
that in ancient Scotland, when a ship became

unmanageable, lots were cast to discover who occasioned the disaster—precisely as in the case of Jonah and in that of the Undutiful Daughter, and the man on whom the lot fell was cast overboard.

In an old English broadside ballad,—

> They had not sailed a league, but three,
> Till raging grew the roaring sea;
> There rose a tempest in the skies,
> Which filled our hearts with great surprise.
> The sea did wash, both fore and aft,
> Till scarce one sail on board was left;
> Our yards were split, and our rigging tore,
> The like was never seen before.
> The boatswain then he did declare
> The captain was a murderer,
> Which did enrage the whole ship's crew;
> Our captain overboard we threw.

It is but a step from drowning a man as an offering to the hungry sea to allowing a man to drown, refusing him help, as was the case in Orkney and Shetland and in Cornwall as well. On the west coast of Ireland, when the Spanish sailors were wrecked from the Armada, the Irish murdered and threw them back into the sea, not that they bore them animosity —these Spaniards were Roman Catholics as well as the Irishmen, but because it was unlucky to rescue any one from the sea, which exacts its toll of human life. It is not only the sea that makes these demands, but, as we have seen, rivers as well. So do lakes.

On Dartmoor is a sheet of water in a depression, called Classenwell pool, covering about an acre of ground. It has been dug out of the southern part of the hill and along the verge of the banks on the tors; the measurement is three hundred and forty-six yards. From this part, which is level with the adjacent common, the banks slope rapidly down to the margin of the pool. On the east side the bank is almost perpendicular, and is nearly one hundred feet high. According to popular superstition a voice can be heard at night shouting a name of some inhabitant of the parish of Walkhampton, in which it is situated, several times and on successive nights, when that individual is certain to obey the call by death.

Now let us consider another current of popular superstition. At the foundation of any building—a church, a town hall, a private mansion—almost invariably a coin is laid beneath the foundation stone. The coin takes the place of an animal. I will not enter fully into this, because I have dealt with it at large elsewhere.[1] But I will mention the salient facts. There can be no doubt that in the early Middle Ages a horse, a lamb, or a dog was laid under the foundations. In

[1] *Strange Survivals.* 3rd ed. Methuen & Co. 1905.

Devonshire almost every church had its
ghostly beast which guarded the church and
churchyard. In the parish of Lew Trenchard
it was two white pigs yoked together with
a silver chain. In an adjoining parish it was
a black dog. In another it was a calf. In
Denmark the church lamb was a constant
apparition. But the burial of an animal
under a foundation stone was a substitution
for a human victim.

In 1885 Holsworthy Church in Devon was
restored, and in the course of restoration the
south-west angle wall of the church was taken
down. In it, embedded in the mortar and
stone, was found a skeleton. The wall of
this portion of the church was faulty, and
had settled. According to the account given
by the masons who found the ghastly remains,
and of the architect who superintended the
work, there was no trace of a tomb, but every
appearance of the person having been buried
alive, and hurriedly. A mass of mortar was
over the mouth, and the stones were huddled
about the corpse as though hastily heaped about
it; then the wall was leisurely proceeded with.

In the Eifel district, rising out of a gorge,
is a ridge on which stand the ruins of two
castles, Ober and Nieder Manderscheid.
According to popular tradition, a young

damsel was built into the wall of Nieder
Manderscheid. In 1844 the wall at this point
was broken down, and a cavity revealed
itself, in the depth of the wall, in which a
human skeleton actually was discovered.

The Baron of Winneberg, in the Eifel,
ordered a master mason to erect a strong
tower whilst he was absent. On his return
he found that the tower had not been built,
and he threatened to dismiss the mason.
The man, in order to fulfil his engagement,
laid his own child in the wall and reared the
tower over her.

When a few years ago the bridge gate of
Bremen was demolished, the skeleton of a
child was actually found embedded in the
foundation. Many years ago, when the ram-
parts were being raised round Copenhagen,
the wall always sank, so that it was not possible
to get it to stand firm. They therefore took
a little innocent girl, placed her in a chair
by a table, and gave her playthings. While
she was thus enjoying herself twelve masons
built an arch over her, which, when completed,
was closed up, and she was immured alive.

Sir Walter Scott, in his notes to the ballad
of the *Cout of Keeldar*, alludes to the tradition that the foundation stones of Pictish
raths were bathed in human gore. Heinrich

Heine says on the subject : 'In the Middle
Ages the opinion prevailed that when any
building was to be erected, something living
must be killed, in the blood of which the
foundation had to be laid, by which process
the building would be secured from falling;
and in ballads and traditions the remembrance
is still preserved how that children and animals
were slaughtered for the purpose of strengthen-
ing large buildings with blood.'

We come now to the consideration as to
whence came these traditions of human
sacrifice—whether to the corn, or the sea;
to the river, or to the earth.

There can exist no doubt that the Aryan
race did practise human sacrifice.    The
Greeks, the Latins, the Germans, and Scandinavians, the Celts and the Sclaves all
practised these horrible rites.    But with all
of them, if I mistake not, the notion was the
same as with the Semitic—that the offering
was made to an offended God, and that it
was expiatory.

But with the Dravidians in India, and with
those of the primitive race in Europe and
in Great Britain, no such a conception
probably existed.    In fact, those who burnt
a lamb or a bull, or refused to enable a drowning man to escape, or who buried an animal

under a foundation stone, had no notion whatever as to any Being to whom the offering was made. I have spoken with those who have been engaged in such rites, and have assured myself that they have believed only in the sacrifice being remedial, but have had no thought of it as an oblation to any deity or devil. When the English officers visited the Khonds, they were so full of the Aryan idea of sacrifice that they took for granted that the butchery of victims was an offering to the Earth goddess. But I am quite convinced that the Khonds had no conception of the sort, any more than my sidesman had when he sacrificed a white cock to avert a murrain.[1]

The men of the Ivernian race had not reached a higher plane of thought than the personification of Death and Life, and that but imperfectly. The Corn Spirit was but a vague idea. It could be killed when driven into the last shock of wheat. There was no conception of a Ceres, an ever-living goddess of the Harvest.

The field demanded blood, the sea a human victim, the earth a buried child—but the field was a dead, dumb object unpersonified;

[1] In my *Strange Superstitions*, written in 1891, I was obsessed by the idea of sacrifice to the Earth Goddess. This I reject now.

so was the sea—it was the sea, not Neptune;
the earth was earth and no more.  The sun,
the moon, the stars made their revolutions,
but received no worship; they were dis-
regarded by the autocthones.  And if we have
amongst us so many reminiscences of the
religion, such as it was—superstition rather—
of the prehistoric Ivernian race, it is because
we have in our midst the descendants of
that race, with their intelligence but very
slightly raised above that of their primeval
ancestors.

## CHAPTER VI

### THE MYSTERY OF DEATH

A few years ago I was planning a dolmen (in
English usually, but incorrectly, called a
cromlech) near Brives, in the department of
Corrèze, when the local antiquary, M. Philibert
Lalande, informed me that it had been
excavated, and on that occasion a curious
fact had been revealed.  It contained half
a skeleton.  The upper half had been incinerated and was enclosed in a pot; but from
the waist downward there had been carnal
interment; above the feet were bronze anklets
that had stained the bones green.  Clearly

there had been a domestic quarrel over this lady's corpse—for that of a female it was. Some desired to have her cremated, according to the last new fashion; whereas others preferred following the ancestral usage of interment of the dead body. At length they split the difference by sawing the good woman in half, with each party disposing of their share in the manner most consonant to their opinions. Of one thing there can exist no manner of doubt : that carnal interment was the original custom of that prehistoric race that, for want of a better name, we designate Ivernian; and that the cremating of the dead came in with the Aryan conquerors or settlers.

These two methods of disposing of corpses indicate divergence of sentiment relative to death.

The supposition that death was the complete annihilation of the living, the thought that any human being who to-day is a dweller full of joy and vigour in our midst, could possibly be absolutely extinct to-morrow, such a notion was utterly and entirely foreign to the mind of prehistoric man, as it is to the savage of to-day. The earliest and rudest conception of death is that of suspended animation, like sleep or a fit. Lartet has described to us the sepulchral cave of Aurignac in the Pyrenees, in which were found human skeletons of the post-glacial date, showing tokens of reverent burial, with rude stone weapons laid ready for their use, and provisions supplied for their entertainment, as also remains of funeral feasts at the cave's mouth.

In the vast American continent, in which tribes are widely scattered and isolated, many in a state of lowest barbarism, the belief in a continuance of life after death is general; and the dead warrior is buried with his most useful weapons and choicest ornaments. Even the babe, whose life is usually accounted of little value among savages, was buried by the careful mother with precious strings of wampum that had occupied her busy fingers more months of patient toil than the days of the infant's short life. Among the rude stone monument builders, whose huge *allées couvertes* in the north-west of France, in Ireland, in Denmark, and Southern Sweden are our wonder to-day, these immense structures, reared at the cost of enormous labour, were dwelling-houses for the dead. In life these megalithic monument builders were content to squat in small bee-hive huts, in which they could not stand

upright.   But for the dead, they reared
palaces.   These were not abodes for the
invisible soul, but for the bodies.   And for
the bodies food was supplied.   Most of these
structures have either a movable slab as
door, or else one perforated, through which
meals for the deceased might be passed.

On the Causse above Terrasson, in Dor-
dogne, is a dolmen with a cuplike hollow in
the capstone.   A friend of mine living near
learned that the peasants were wont to place
either money or meal or grapes in it.   So
one night he concealed himself within the
cist.   Presently a peasantess came and
deposited a *sou* in the cavity, when my
friend roared out in patois : 'Ce n'est pas
assez.   Donnez moi encore !'   Whereupon
the woman emptied her purse into the
receptacle and fled.

In North Devon, at Washfield, the squire,
a Mr Worth, was a sportsman.   When he
died, in the eighteenth century, he gave
orders that his hounds should be slaughtered
and buried with him.   The dogs were indeed
killed, but interred outside the churchyard
wall.   At the funeral of a cavalry officer or
a general, his horse is led in the procession,
and is slightly wounded in the frog of one
hoof, so as to oblige it to limp.   Originally

the horse was killed and buried with the warrior, and our usage is the faint trace of the old barbarous custom that has undergone modification.

It is now quite a common practice in England to decorate the graves with flower-wreaths. These take the place of the earlier gifts of food, and show that still in men's minds lingers the pre-Aryan cult of the dead body. The Roman Church has accepted it altogether, and the worship of relics is neither more nor less than the survival of prehistoric beliefs and usage. At Eben, above the Inn Valley, in the church, immediately over the high altar, is a grinning skeleton tricked out with sham flowers and spangles, behind glass. It is the body of St Nothburga; and when the priest is saying mass at the altar, it looks precisely as though he were sacrificing to this skeleton. I have seen many more quite as revolting exhibitions.

There is a curious book entitled *De Miraculis Mortuorum* ('On the Miracles of the Dead'), by a physician, Christian Friderick Garmann, published at Leipzig, 1670. The object of the writer is to refute widely extended beliefs that the dead are still alive in their graves, because the hair and the nails continue to grow after death; because strange sounds and voices have been heard to issue from tombs; because when coffins have been opened the face cloth has been found to have been gnawed, eyes that were closed have opened, children have cut their teeth after death, and so on—some very horrible stories are told. The real interest of the book consists in establishing the fact that in the seventeenth century ideas relative to death pertaining to savages and primeval man prevailed largely in Germany.

Saxo Grammaticus tells us a grim tale. Asmund and Asvid, brothers in arms, had vowed not to be separated in death. It fell out that Asvid died, and was buried along with his horse and dog in a cairn. And Asmund, because of his oath of friendship, had the courage to be buried along with him, food being put in for him to eat. Now just at this time, Eric, King of Sweden, happened to pass nigh the barrow of Asvid, and the Swedes, thinking it might contain treasure, broke into it with mattocks, and came on a vault made of timber. To explore this, a youth was let down in a basket. But Asmund, when he saw the boy descend, cast him out, and got into the basket himself. Then he gave the signal to draw up. Those who drew thought by the weight that the basket contained much treasure.  But when they saw the unknown figure of a man emerge, scared by his strange appearance, and thinking that the dead had come to life again, they flung down the rope and fled.  He tried to recall them, and assured them that they were needlessly alarmed.  And when Eric saw him, he marvelled at the aspect of his bloody face, the blood flowing freely and spurting out.  Then Asmund told his story.  He had been buried with his friend Asvid, but Asvid came to life again every night, and being ravenously hungry, fell on and devoured his horse.  That eaten, he had treated his dog in the same manner; and having consumed that, he turned on his friend, and with his sharp nails tore his cheek and ripped off one of his ears.  Asmund, who had no ambition to be eaten, made a desperate resistance, and finally succeeded in driving a stake through the body of the vampire.

Beginning with the year 1720, there spread through Lower Hungary and Servia and Wallachia a rumour that filled the people with terror ; and this was that vampires were about, sucking the blood of living persons. In 1725 accounts of vampires appeared in the newspapers.  In the village of Kiso-lova died a serf named Peter Posojowitz, and was buried.  Two days later several individuals in the place fell ill, and in eight days nine of them were dead.  Every one of these declared that Peter Posojowitz was the sole cause of their illness.  He had visited them in the night, thrown himself upon them, and sucked their blood.  In order to put a stop to this, the grave was opened at the end of three weeks, and the body was found undecomposed.  The hair, beard, and nails had grown ; the old skin had peeled off, and a fresh skin had formed.  Face and body appeared as sound and healthy as in life.  Fresh blood stained the lips.  The body was taken up, and a stake driven through the heart, whereupon blood spurted from the mouth and ears.  Finally the body was burnt to ashes.

In 1732 appeared the protocol of an investigation made to order by three army surgeons in the presence of the commanding officer of their regiment, into a case of vampirism at Meduegya in Servia.  Five years previously a heyduk named Arnod Paole, living in the place, fell from a hay wagon and broke his neck.  Arnod had in his lifetime often related how that he had been tormented by a vampire in Gossowa.

Some twenty or thirty days after his death several individuals complained that

Arnod Paole had visited them, and four of these died. Accordingly forty days after his burial he was exhumed, and found quite fresh and with blood running out of his eyes, ears, and nostrils. His shirt and shroud were soaked with blood. The old skin and nails had fallen off and fresh had grown. The body was at once burnt. But the mischief was not at an end, for every one who has been bitten by a vampire becomes a vampire as well; and the trouble in Meduegya had become so great that orders were sent by Government to the three surgeons to open all the graves of those who were supposed to have been vampire-bitten, report on their condition, and, if necessary, burn the bodies.

They went accordingly to the cemetery and exhumed thirteen corpses. I can give only briefly a summary of the report, dated January 7, 1732.

1. A woman named Stana, twenty years old, who had died three months previously, after her confinement, along with her child. The latter, having been slovenly buried at insufficient depth, had been half-eaten by dogs. Nevertheless it was supposed to have become a vampire. The body of the mother appeared incorrupt. At the opening of the breast a quantity of fresh extravased blood

was found.  The blood in the cavities of the heart was not coagulated but liquid.  All the internal organs were sound.  The old skin and nails fell off and exposed fresh ones.

2. A woman named Miliza, aged sixty. She had been buried ninety odd days before. Much liquid blood was found in her breast. The viscera and other organs were in the same condition as the last.  But what struck the heyduks standing by, and who had known her for many years, was that in life she had been a thin woman, whereas now she was plump, and under the dissecting knife revealed a strange amount of fat.  She had protested in her last illness that she was the victim of a vampire.

3. An eight-days'-old child which had been ninety days in the earth.  This also in the so-called vampire condition.

4. The son of a heyduk named Milloe, sixteen years old.  The body had been interred nine weeks before.  It was quite sound and in the vampire condition.

5. Joachim, also a heyduk's son, aged seventeen years, had lain in the earth eight weeks and four days.  His body was in the vampire state.

6. A woman named Ruscha had been buried six weeks previously, and her child

eighteen days old, who had been buried five
weeks previously.   Blood found in her breast
and stomach.

7. The same may be said of a girl of ten
who had been laid in the earth two months
before.   She was sound and incorrupt, and
had fresh blood in her bosom.

8. The wife of the present mayor of the
village and her child.   She had died seven
weeks ago and the child twenty-one days
previously.   Both were found in a condition
of corruption though lying in the same earth
and close by the others.

9. A servant of the heyduk, Corporal Rhade
by name, who had lain in the ground five
weeks, undergoing rapid decomposition.

10. A woman buried five weeks before,
also in decomposition.

11. Stanko, a heyduk, sixty years old,
who died six weeks before the investigation.
Much liquid blood in the breast and stomach,
and the whole body in vampire condition.

12. Milloe, a heyduk, twenty-five years old,
buried five weeks before.   In the vampire state.

13. Stanjoika, wife of a heyduk, buried
eighteen days before the examination.   Her
face was rosy.   She had been bitten, so she
had asserted, by Milloe, just mentioned; and
actually on the right side under the ear,

was a blue scar about a finger's length,
with blood about it. At the opening of her
coffin fresh blood ran out of her nostrils, and
there was 'balsamish' blood in the breast and
in the ventricle of the heart. The intestines
were all healthy and sound.

After this visitation all the bodies that
were in vampire condition were beheaded
and then burnt.

A very general belief among the peasantry
of England is—or was—that if a young man
and a young woman are engaged and one of
them dies before they are married, the tie
still subsists, and can be only broken with
difficulty. The dead one may claim the
living. On this is founded Bürger's ballad
of *Leonore*.

I knew a handsome old woman, wife of
a farmer of my neighbourhood in Devon,
who had betrothed herself to a youth in the
place, but he died before the wedding came
off. After a sufficient time had elapsed she
got engaged to the farmer, whom she eventually married. Directly after this the dead
lover appeared to her at night and said :
'Joanna, you cannot marry another than me,
till you have returned my present, the red
silk handkerchief. I'll stop it till I have that
back.' She left her bed and took the kerchief

out of a drawer and handed it to him, whereupon he disappeared.  If remonstrated with,
and told that this was a dream, she would
wax warm and say : 'I know it is true.
I know it, for the silk handkerchief disappeared from that night.  And if you'd ha'
opened his grave you'd ha' found it in his
coffin.'

Sometimes the dead lover insists on taking
away his betrothed, unless she can redeem
herself by answering certain riddles.  There
is a widely-known and sung ballad called
*The Unquiet Grave*.  It begins :—

> Cold blow the winds of night, sweetheart,
>   Cold are the drops of rain.
> The very first love that ever I had,
>   In greenwood he was slain.

The damsel goes to the graveyard and sits
above where he is buried.

> A twelvemonth and a day being up,
>   The ghost began to speak :
> 'Why sit you here, by my graveside,
>   And will not let me sleep?
>         .        .        .
>
> 'What is it that you want of me,
>   And will not let me sleep?
> Your salten tears they trickle down,
>   And wet my winding sheet.'
>
> 'What is it that I want of thee,
>   O what of thee in grave?
> A kiss from off thy lily-white lips,
>   And that is all I crave.'

'Cold are my lips in death, sweetheart,
    My breath is earthy strong;
If you do touch my clay-cold lips,
    Your time will not be long.'

It is, by the way, a mistake to say that 'the ghost began to speak,' for it is obvious from what follows that it is the dead man, and not the ghost at all. The ballad is not complete; there are verses lost. But the gist of it seems to be that the damsel seeks release from her dead lover, and desires to return him the betrothal kiss; but when she finds that there is death in this, she seeks another solution, and is set tasks.

'Go fetch me a light from dungeon deep,
    Wring water from a stone,
And likewise milk from a maiden's breast
    That never babe had none.'

She stroke a light from out a flint,
    An ice-bell (icicle) squeezed she,
And pressed the milk from a Johnis wort,
    And so she did all three.

'Now if you were not true in word,
    As now I know you be,
I'd tear you as the withered leaves
    Are torn from off the tree.'

There used to be played in farm-houses in Cornwall a dialogue game of this kind. The dead lover goes outside the door, comes in and threatens to carry off the damsel who is

seated in the middle of the room.  She objects
to go.  Then he says that he will only give up
his rights to her if she will accomplish certain
tasks.

> Go fetch me, my lady, a cambric shirt,
>     Whilst every grove rings with a merry
>         antine (*antienne*),
> And stitch it without any needlework,
>     And thou shalt be a true lover of mine.
>
> O thou must wash it in yonder well,
> Where never a drop of water in fell;
> O thou must bleach it on yonder grass,
> Where never a foot or a hoof did pass.
>
> And thou must hang it upon a white thorn,
> That never blossomed since Adam was born.
> Unless[1] these works are finished and done,
> I'll take and marry thee under the sun.

To this the girl replies :—

> Thou must buy for me an acre of land,
> Between the salt sea and the yellow sand.
>
> Thou must plough it o'er with a horse's horn,
> And sow it over with a peppercorn.
>
> Thou must reap it, too, with a piece of leather,
> And bind it up with a peacock's feather.
>
> Thou must take it up in a bottomless sack,
> And bear it to mill on a butterfly's back.
>
> And when these works are finished and done,
> I'll take and marry thee under the sun.

[1] As I took the song down, this line ran 'And when,'
but clearly it should be 'Unless.'

'In all stories of this kind,' says Professor Child, 'the person upon whom a task is imposed stands acquitted if another of no less difficulty is devised which must be performed first.'

Among the Bretons, when a young couple are engaged, they go to the graves of their parents and grandparents, and announce the fact to them. In all these cases the dead are supposed to be in a comatose state, and there is no thought of the soul as apart from the body.

But there have existed ideas concerning the intercourse between the dead and the living still more close. The classic story of the Bride of Corinth formed the basis of a not over pleasant ballad by Goethe. A similar idea is found in Iceland.

Helgi Hundingsbane was visited in his grave-mound by his wife Sigrun, who spent a night there with him. He informed her that all her tears fell on and moistened him. 'Here, Helgi,' said she, 'have I prepared for thee in thy mound a peaceful bed. On thy breast, chieftain, will I repose as I was wont in thy lifetime.' To which the dead Helgi replies: 'Nothing is to be regarded as unexpected, since thou, living, a king's daughter, sleepest in a grave-mound in the arms of a corpse.'

In some cases the devil has taken the place
of a dead man.  This would appear to be
what has happened in the following story,
taken down by me verbatim from an old
woman in the parish of Luffincott in North
Devon.   I will give it in her own words:—
'There was an old woman lived in Bridgerule
parish, and she had a very handsome daughter.
One evening a carriage and four drove to the
door, and a gentleman stepped out.  He was
a fine-looking man, and he made some excuse
to stay in the cottage talking, and he made
love to the maiden, and she was rather taken
with him.   Then he drove away, but next
evening he came again, and it was just the
same thing;  and he axed the maid if on the
third night she would go in the coach with
him, and be married.  She said Yes; and he
made her swear that she would.

'Well, the old mother did not think that all
was quite right, so she went to the pars'n
of Bridgerule and axed he about it.  "My
dear," said he, "I reckon it's the Old Un.
Now, look y' here.  Take this 'ere candle,
and ax that gen'leman next time he comes
to let your Polly alone till this 'ere candle be
burnt out.  Then take it, blow it out, and rin
along on all your legs to me."

'So the old woman took the candle.

'Next night the gen'leman came in his carriage and four, and he went into the cottage and axed the maid to come wi' he, as she'd sworn and promised. She said, "I will, but you must give me a bit o' time to dress myself." He said, "I'll give you till thickey candle be burnt out."

'Now, when he had said this, the old woman blew the candle out and rinned away as fast as she could, right on end to Bridgerule, and the pars'n he tooked the can'l and walled it up in the side o' the church; you can see where it be to this day (it is the rood loft staircase upper door, now walled up). Well, when the gen'leman saw he was done, he got into his carriage and drove away, and he drove till he comed to Affaland Moor, and then all to wance down went the carriage and horses and all into a sort o' bog there, and blue flames came up all round where they went down.'

The conversion of a dead lover into the devil is obviously a Christianised modification of a very ancient belief, that the dead do come and claim female companions. In all likelihood there lingered on a tradition of some gentleman having been engulfed in the morass of Affaland.

One more story, and that very significant,

as it shows that even in modern times belief exists in the dead being in a condition of suspended animation in their graves. It is recorded by the late Mr Elworthy. 'Not long ago, I met Farmer——, who lives on a farm belonging to me in Devonshire. After the usual salutations, the following conversation occurred :—

'*Farmer :* "I s'pose you've a-yeard th' old 'umman —— is dead to last."

'*F. T. E. :* "No, I had not heard of it. Where did she die? Not in this parish, I hope. She was here living not very long ago."

'*Farmer :* "Oh, no; her wid'n bide here. Her zaid how they was trying to pwoisen her, so her made 'em take her home, and they drawed her home in a carriage. Her was that wicked, her died awful. Her died cussin' and dam'in'—wi' the words in her mouth."

'*F. T. E. :* "Poor thing ! I suppose she was mad. When did she die?"

'*Farmer :* "Her died last Monday, and her's going to be buried t'arternoon to Culmstock."

'*F. T. E. :* "It's a good thing for us she is not going to be buried here, for she's sure to be troublesome wherever she lies."

'*Farmer :* "Oh no, her 'ont, sir. You knows Joe, don't 'ee, sir? Well, I seed Joe this morning, and he's gwain to help car' her;

so I sez to Joe, say I, 'For God's sake, Joe, be sure and put her in up'm down.' "

'*F. T. E.:* "Do you mean that the coffin is to be turned upside down?"

'*Farmer:* "Ay, sure, and no mistake! Her 'ont be troublesome then, 'cause if her do begin to diggy, her can on'y diggy downwards."

Mr Elworthy adds: 'I have known other cases of interments that have been made face downwards.'

Now Frobenius, in *The Childhood of Man*, says that on the Shari River that flows into Lake Tchad in Central Africa, on a death they 'make a breach in the walls of the hut, through which the blindfolded body, face downwards and head foremost, is carried out, the breach being then again closed up. The people of the Shari explain that they turn the body face down and bandage the eyes to prevent the spirit from knowing which way the body was taken.' Frobenius is here a little mistaken. This treatment of the body is in order to prevent the *body* from returning and being vexatious to its relatives.

All these superstitions pertain to very early conceptions of death, of a period when carnal interment was practised.

In the year 1779 there were living together

two widows, sisters, and the daughter of one
of them, at a farm called Blackabroom, in the
parish of Bratton Clovelly in Devon, when a
man, a tramp, called and asked for food. They
gave him his tea, after which he murdered all
three,[1] and searched the house for money, but
found only £5, as the rest had been securely concealed. The man, whose name was Welland,
went into Hatherleigh, where he betrayed himself by unguarded talking about the murder.
He was arrested and hung in chains on Broad-
bury Down, a crescent of high land covered
with heather, and where lie many tumuli. The
gallows tree is still in existence in a barn near.
Now I believe it to be an absolute fact, that
till the body fell to pieces, the women coming
home from market every Saturday were wont
to throw up to him a bunch of tallow candles
for him to eat, and they generally succeeded
in getting the dips to catch in his chains. As
the candles disappeared during the week—
pecked by birds—the women concluded that
Welland had actually fed on them. Obviously

---

[1] Extract from Burial Register, Bratton Clovelly:—

BURIALS, 1779.

1. Grace Peard, widow, was buried  .  Nov. 5.
2. Patience Rundle, widow  .    .  Nov. 5.
8. Mary Rundle, daughter of Wm.
    and Patience Rundle  .    .  Nov. 5.

These 8 ware Barbibly murdered.
        *sic*  *sic*
[In very small obscure writing underneath.]

the idea was still prevalent that life continued to exist in the body after execution. The gallows was standing in 1814.

In 1832 occurred a great rising of the peasantry in Hungary against the nobles. It was ruthlessly put down, and fifty Slovack peasants were hung on gallows in different parts. Curiously enough, every New Year's Day, each body was afforded by the relatives a new suit of clothes. (Paget, *Hungary and Transylvania*, 1850, I., p. 432.)

Here again, clearly the dead are supposed to be still alive, after a fashion.

Two farmers in the neighbourhood of Cologne, living in the same village, were at enmity with each other all their days. During an epidemic both died within a few hours of each other, and as burials were many, a double grave was dug, and the two men were put in, back to back. Thereupon the two corpses began kicking at each other with their heels, and it was found necessary to take out one of them and dig for him a fresh grave.

After a while at an early period a complete change in observance ensued. Carnal interment was abandoned, and the dead were burned. In consequence, no more huge dolmens and halls of stone slabs were erected, and the ashes of the deceased were enclosed in a pot over which a small kistvaen was erected.

With the burning of the dead the old belief in the bodies of the departed walking, requiring food, sucking blood, claiming brides, suffered eclipse, only to return full again with Christianity, when bodies were once more interred.

With incineration, the ghost took the place of the restless body.

The change from burying the body to burning it was due to a revolt of the living against the tyranny and exactions of the dead. The dead having been treated very handsomely, made themselves, as Devonshire people would put it, 'proper nuisances.' They meddled in private affairs, would have the best cut off the joint, and the last bit of fashionable finery; they insisted on being periodically visited, their bones scraped, and their skulls polished. Falling into a morbid condition of mind, men were continually seeing phantoms in sleep and awake—to such an extent that those who were in this condition could not distinguish between what they had dreamt and what they had actually seen. A modern observer's description of the state of mind of the negroes of South

Guinea in this respect would apply to that of the dolmen builders of old. 'All their dreams are construed into visits from the spirits of their deceased friends. The cautions, hints, and warnings that come to them through this source are received with the most serious and deferential attention, and are always acted upon in their waking hours. The habit of relating their dreams, which is universal, greatly promotes the habit of dreaming itself, and hence their sleeping hours are characterised by almost as much intercourse with the dead as their waking are with the living. Their imaginations become so lively that they can scarcely distinguish between their dreams and their waking thoughts, between the real and the ideal, and they consequently utter falsehood without intending, and profess to see things which never existed.'

No evidence exists that the change of custom from carnal inhumation to incineration was due to external influence, to contact with another people who burned instead of burying their dead. The same weapons and ornaments and pottery are found in the cairns that cover the ashes of the dead as in the rude stone chambers in which they were laid unburned. It was due to the impatience

of the living to escape from the thraldom
of the dead that the revolution in practice
took place. This is not mere conjecture, for
it can be shown to have taken place in
historic times. Among the Scandinavians
interment of the dead was usual ; but should
a departed individual become troublesome, he
was dug up and burnt.

The classical instance is that of Glamr in
the Grettis Saga. I have told the story elsewhere[1] so fully that I can but give an outline
of it here.

Early in the eleventh century a farm stood
in a valley that leads into the Vatnsdale in
Northern Iceland. I have seen its foundations.
In this lived a man named Thorhall. His
sheep-walks were haunted, and his shepherds
murdered by being strangled or their backs
broken. It was ascertained that the cause of
this was that a certain Glamr who had been
in the service of Thorhall 'walked,' not
only about the farm but even over the roof
of the house, and one night broke into it.
Grettir the Strong, who was staying with
Thorhall, put a stop to these unpleasantnesses
by first snapping the spine of the corpse and
then burning it to ashes. That done, the
charred remains were conveyed many miles

[1] A Book of Ghosts. Methuen & Co., London.

inland into the desert and there buried
under a cairn of stones; and I have seen and
sketched that same cairn.

This is not a solitary instance. Several
others are related to the same effect. Corpses
were left in their graves to sleep in peace,
but if they became troublesome they were
incinerated. What took place in Iceland on
a small scale took place on a large one among
the dolmen builders, and for the same reason.
We have seen the same system adopted in
the case of the vampires in Servia so late as
1732.

Popular superstition now oscillated between
the two conceptions of death. We have seen
a Devonshire farmer entertain precisely the
same notions relative to a corpse that are
found among savages almost at the bottom
of the cultural ladder. But undoubtedly
the legacy from the age of incineration, the
idea of the spirit detached from and independent of the body manifesting itself, is the most
prevalent.

There was a woman at Horbury Bridge,
near Wakefield, who kept a little shop. We
had many a long talk together, and she told
me two stories of her experiences that show
that the two independent conceptions relative
to death were in her mind.

A woman had died in the house, and the body was put in a shell in the room over the kitchen, where she and a friend were sitting. All at once both of them heard a noise overhead, as if the corpse were getting out of its coffin, and this was followed by steps on the floor. The two women listened in alarm, till they heard the dead body return to its former place, when they ventured upstairs. The corpse was in its shell, but the linen that had enfolded it was rumpled, and some flowers that had lain on the bosom were displaced.

The other story was this. When this good woman was a girl of sixteen her mother died, and she went into a situation in the same hamlet, where she was very unhappy because unkindly treated. One night she left the house, ran to the churchyard, and, kneeling by her mother's grave, told her the tale of her sorrows. Then she saw the vaporous form of her mother standing or floating above the grave-mound. As the woman described it, it was as if made out of fog and moonshine, but the face was distinct. And she heard the apparition say : 'Bear up, Bessie, lass ! It's no but for a little while, and then thou'lt be right.' Whereat the figure slowly dissolved and disappeared.

The belief in ghosts is so prevalent, so widely extended, and so many more or less authentic stories of their appearances exist, that a thick book might be filled with them. What is more to the point is that though most educated individuals repudiate the notion, they nevertheless retain a sneaking conviction that there may be some truth in the many stories that they hear; and they endeavour to explain them on natural grounds. All these stories derive from the period when men burnt their dead, and so put an end to the conception of the continued life after death of dead bodies.

I have already mentioned the doctrine of metempsychosis, brought with the Aryans from the East, their first home. But along with the notion that human souls after death passed into some other body, there were other explanations given as to what became of disembodied souls.

One was that they wandered in the wind ; the moaning, the screaming, and the piping of the blast was set down to the voices of the souls, bewailing their fate as excluded from shelter under a roof and a seat by the fireside.

> The wind blows cold on waste and wold,
>   It bloweth night and day.
> The souls go by 'twixt earth and sky,
>   Impatient not to stay.

> They fly in clouds and flap their shrouds,
>   When full the moon doth sail;
> In dead of night, when lacketh light,
>   We hear them sob and wail.
>
> And many a soul with dismal howl
>   Doth rattle at the door,
> Or rave and rout, with dance and shout
>   Around the granite tor.
> We hear a soul i' th' chimney growl
>   That's drenched with the rain,
> To wring the wet from winding sheet,
>   To feel the fire 't were fain.

This idea is not antagonistic to metempsychosis: it shows us the spirits of the deceased wandering over the world in quest of bodies that they may occupy. In African tribes a madman is supposed to be possessed of two souls, one of a lately deceased man that has taken up its abode in him, the other is his own spirit. Frobenius mentions a case. 'A few years ago such a possessed person burnt a whole village in the Gaboon district without any one preventing him. The villagers stood by and looked on, not venturing even to save their own effects. When the Government forces arrived, there was a great row, and the arrest of the poor idiot almost led to a war.'

In Yorkshire, Essex, and on Dartmoor it is supposed that the souls that pipe and wail on the wind are those of unbaptized children.  Usually such ghosts as are reported to have been seen are those of persons who have committed some crime, or suicide, but also occasionally those of victims who have been murdered and have not received Christian burial.

As peoples became more civilised and thought more deeply of the mystery of death, they conceived of a place where the souls lived on, and being puzzled to account for the rainbow, came to the conclusion that it was a bridge by means of which spirits mounted to their abode above the clouds. The Milky Way was called variously the Road of the Gods or the Road of Souls. Among the Norsemen, after Odin had constructed his heavenly palace, aided by the dwarfs, he reared the bridge Bifröst, which men call the Rainbow, by which it could be reached.  It is of three colours: that in the middle is red, and is of fire, to consume any unworthy souls that would venture up the bridge.  In connection with this idea of a bridge uniting heaven and earth, up which souls ascended, arose the custom of persons constructing bridges for the good of the souls of their kinsfolk.  On runic grave-stones in Denmark and Sweden we find such inscriptions as these: 'Nageilfr had this bridge

built for Anund, his good son.' 'The mother
built the bridge for her only son.' 'Holdfast had the bridge constructed for Hame, his
father, who lived in Viby.' 'Holdfast had the
road made for Igul and for Ura, his dear
wife.' At Sundbystein, in the Uplands, is an
inscription showing that three brothers and
sisters erected a bridge over a ford for their
father.

The bridge as a means of passage for the
soul from this earth to eternity must have
been known also to the Ancients, for in the
Cult of Demeter, the goddess of Death, at
Eleusis, where her mysteries were gone
through, in order to pass at once after death
into Elysium, there was an order of Bridge
priestesses; and the goddess bore the name of
the Lady of the Bridge. In Rome also the
priest was a bridge-builder *pontifex*, as he
undertook the charge of souls. In Austria
and parts of Germany it is still supposed
that children's souls are led up the rainbow to
heaven. Both in England and among the
Chinese it is regarded as a sin to point with
the finger at the bow. With us no trace of
the idea that it is a Bridge of Souls remains.
Probably this was thought to be a heathen
belief and was accordingly forbidden, for
children in the North of England to this day,

when a rainbow appears, make a cross on the ground with a couple of twigs or straws, 'to cross out the bow.' The West Riding recipe for driving away a rainbow is: 'Make a cross of two sticks and lay four pebbles on it, one at each end.'

A more common notion as to the spirits of the dead was the shipping of them to a land in the West, where the sun goes down—Hy Brazil, as the Irish called it.

In Yorkshire, North and East Riding, the clouds at even sometimes take the form of a ship, and the people call it Noah's Ark, and observe if it points Humber-ways as a weather prognostic. Although I have never heard them say that it was a soul-ship, I have little doubt that originally it was supposed to be such. Noah's Ark was not empty. There is a story in Gervase of Tilbury that leads to this surmise. The book, *Otia Imperialia*, was written in 1211.

On a certain feast-day in Great Britain, when the congregations came pouring out of church, they saw to their surprise an anchor let down from above the clouds, attached to a rope. The anchor caught in a tombstone; and though those above shook the cable repeatedly, they could not disengage it. Then the people heard voices above the clouds discussing apparently the propriety of sending some one down to release the flukes of the anchor, and shortly after they saw a sailor swarming down the cable. Before he could release the anchor he was laid hold of ; he gasped and collapsed, as though drowning in the heavy air about the earth. After waiting about an hour, those in the aerial vessel cut the rope, and it fell down. The anchor was hammered out into the hinges and straps of the church door, where, according to Gervase, they were to be seen in his day. Unfortunately he does not tell us the name of the place where they are to be seen.

Agobard, Bishop of Lyons, who died in 840, wrote against the superstitions prevalent in his day, and he says that he had heard and seen many persons who believed that there was a country called Magonia, whence sailed ships among the clouds, manned by aerial sailors, who took on board grain and fruit from off the earth, and poured down hail and sent tempests.

That the cloud vessel is the Ship of Souls is made clear by certain extant Cornish traditions. I will quote instances from Hunt's *Romances and Drolls of the West of England*, and Bottrell's *Traditions of West Cornwall*.

A phantom ship was seen approaching

against wind and tide, sailing over land and sea in a cloudy squall, and in it departed the soul of a wrecker. His last moments were terrible, a tempest taking place in the room, where the plashing of water was heard. A similar spectral barque occurs in another story. 'These caverns and cleaves were all shrouded in mist, which seemed to be gathering from all quarters to that place, till it formed a black cloud above and a thick haze below, out of which soon appeared the black masts of a black ship scudding away to sea, with all her sails set, and not a breath of wind stirring.' It carried off the soul of a noted white witch.

A story told at Priest's Cove is much like these. Here a pirate lived. At his death a cloud came up, with a square-rigged ship in it, and the words, 'The hour is come, but not the man,' were heard. As the ship sailed over the house, the dying man's room was filled with the noise of waves and breakers, and the house shook as the soul of the wrecker passed away, borne in the cloud ship.

In Porthcurno harbour spectral ships are believed to be seen sailing over land and sea.

Near Penrose a spectral boat, laden with smugglers, was believed to be seen passing at

times over the moors, in an equally spectral
sea and a driving fog. By degrees, not always
in the same place nor at any fixed period, the
idea of the Ship of Souls in the clouds material-
ised into actual boats in which the spirits of
the dead were carried over, not to a mystical
land of Magonia, but to actual islands or
territories.

The western coast of Brittany, with its
sheer granite cliffs starting out of an ever-
boiling sea, but with its strange inland wave-
less lakes of the Morbihan and the Gulf of
Etel, and with its desolate wind-swept wolds,
strewn with prehistoric monuments of the
dead, more numerous than anywhere else, has
been esteemed the gathering-place of souls
seeking to be shipped either to the Isles of
the Blessed, or to Britia, that is none other
than Great Britain.

No place could have been selected more
suitable for the purpose than the Pointe de
Raz. Near it is the Bay of Souls. The rising
and falling ground is barren. Here is the
Tarn of Cleden, about which the skeletons
of drowned men congregate and run after
a stranger, imploring him to give them a
winding-sheet and a grave.

Procopius, who died shortly after 543,
tells us how that hence the souls of the

departed are shipped across to the Island
Britia.   Near the coast are some islands
inhabited by fishermen, tradesmen, and ferrymen.   These often cross over to Britain on
trading affairs intent.   Although they are
under the Frank crown, they pay no taxes,
and none are required of them.   The reason
is that it is their office to ferry over the souls
of the dead to the places appointed for their
residence.   Those whose obligation it is in
the ensuing night to discharge this duty go
to bed as soon as darkness sets in and snatch
as much sleep as they can.   About midnight
a tap is heard at the door, and they are called
in a low voice.   Immediately they rise and
run down to the coast, without well knowing
what mysterious cause of attraction draws
them thither.   Here they find their boats
apparently empty, yet actually so laden that
the water is up to the bulwarks, hardly a
finger's breadth above the surface.   In less
than an hour they bring their boats across
to Great Britain, whereas ordinarily a ship
with stout and continuous rowing would not
reach it in a day and a half.   As soon as
they have reached the British shore, the
souls leave the ships, and these at once rise
in the sea, as though wholly without lading.
The boatmen return home without having seen

any one either when going or when discharging their freight. But, as they testify, they can hear a voice on the shore calling out the names of those who are to disembark with those of their parents, their followers, and their character. When women's souls are on board, then the names of their husbands are given.

Claudian also had heard this story, but he confused the northern shipping of the dead with the nether world practices when Ulysses descended. On the extreme coast of Gaul is a place sheltered from the ocean, where Ulysses by sacrifice summoned the spirits of the dead about him. There he could hear the faint wailing of the vaporous spirits that surrounded him, forms like the dead on their travels.

There are numerous German stories of ferrymen shipping invisible fares over the Rhine, the Weser, and the Elbe.

The Greeks and Romans believed in the Elysian fields knee-deep in asphodels, where wandered souls, and to which they were ferried across the river of Styx by Charon.

Now let us examine the genesis of these beliefs.

The conception of a region of the gods above the clouds, to which access was had by the rainbow bridge, is not primitive.

The Norsemen were Vikings who raided up the Rhine, the Seine, the Loire; who pushed down to the Garonne, to Spain, and through the Straits into the Mediterranean and reached Constantinople, where some of them took service under the Greek Emperors. Insensibly their ideas of cosmogony got influenced by the Christians with whom they were brought in continual contact; and they adopted the notion of a heaven of the gods above the clouds. But this was not their original belief. They held that the world was round and flat, and that about it flowed a mighty river. Beyond this was Gloesisvellir, the Shining Plains, to which the dead were shipped. These ideas got localised. The Celts had their convictions that the Land of the Spirits was beyond the setting sun, and St Brendan and his party sailed in a carack in quest of it, but failed to discover it. In Germany the localisation of the Land of Souls was across one of the broad rivers. In the confusion of ideas some held that a heavenly ship among or above the clouds transported the souls to their final home. But this theory was not lasting. Still, it existed.

At first the Aryan idea was metempsychosis. Then as the souls could not find bodies to animate, they went wandering in quest of them.   Next they formed the notion that across the sea, or the river that flowed round the earth, the souls went in boats.

And now we find this notion by no means extinct.   Hamlet says :—

> (Age) hath shipped me into the land
> As if I had never been such.

And there is a hymn issued by the Sunday School Union, and sung up and down the land :—

> Shall we meet beyond the river,
>   Where the surges cease to roll?
> Where in all the bright for ever
>   Sorrow ne'er shall vex the soul.
>
> Shall we meet with many dear ones
>   Who were torn from our embrace?
> Shall we listen to their voices,
>   And behold them face to face?

This is old Paganism wearing a Christian mask.

The ancient Greeks put on their tombs the word *Euploia*, 'Favourable voyage,' showing the popular ideas on the subject.   For this, modern Greeks substitute a pair of oars laid on the grave.

Mannhardt was quite right in saying : 'From the afore-recorded customs and stories it appears abundantly clear that the traversing of souls across water is deeply grounded in the consciousness of the people. As this is also found among the Celts, the Greeks, the Irish, and in the Hindu religions, it is apparent that this conception goes back to a period before the separation of the several branches of the stock.'

King Arthur was carried away in a boat after the battle in which he received his death-wound to Avalon, the Isle of Apples, that was identified afterwards with Glastonbury.

Now let us look at the final phase of this notion of the shipping of the dead, and this we discover in the myth of the Flying Dutchman.

The earliest trace of this I find in the Greek *Acts of Saints Adrian and Natalia.* Adrian was martyred about the year 804, but the *Acts* are much later. After the death of Adrian, at Nicomedia, his wife Natalia took ship to go to Byzantium.

As the vessel was on its way, storm and darkness came on, and out of the gloom shot a phantom ship filled with dark forms. The steersman of Natalia's vessel shouted to the captain of the phantom ship for sailing directions, not knowing in the darkness and mist that this vessel was not real and freighted with living men. Then a tall black form at

the poop shouted through the flying spindrift,
'To the left, to the left; lean over to the left !'
and so the steersman turned the prow.    At
that instant a luminous figure stood out in
the night, at the head of the vessel, with a
halo about him such as we see encircle a
lantern in a fog.    It was Adrian in glory.
And he waved his arm and cried, 'You are
sailing aright !    Go straight forward.'    And
Natalia uttered a cry and sprang forward,
crying, 'It is my husband—it is Adrian come
to save us !'

Then the light vanished and all was dark.
The storm blew down on them, laden with
the shrieks of the discomfited demons, as
the black fiend-ship backed into the gloom.
Here, as a matter of course, in a saintly legend,
the souls of bad men in the phantom ship
become devils.

The next story of which I am aware is one
that purported to be from an old manuscript
not older than the sixteenth century, and probably of the seventeenth, that appeared in
the *Morgenblatt* for 1824.    'Whilst we were
sailing from the Rio de Plata for Spain, one
night I heard a cry, "A sail !"    I ran at once
on deck, but saw nothing.    The man who kept
watch looked greatly disturbed.    When I
spoke to him, he explained the reason of his

condition.  Looking out, he had seen a black frigate sail by so close that he could see the figurehead, which represented a skeleton with a spear in his right hand.  He also saw the crew on deck, which resembled the figurehead, only that skin was drawn over their bones.  Their eyes were sunk deep in the sockets, and had in them a stare like that of dead bodies.  Nevertheless they handled the cordage and managed the sail, which latter was so thin as to be like cobwebs, and the stars could be dimly seen through them.  The only word he heard, as the mysterious barque glided by, was "Water."  The man who had seen this became depressed through the rest of the voyage and died soon after.'

There are various versions of the story framed to account for the vision of the Flying Dutchman.  That most usually accepted is that an unbelieving Dutch captain had vainly tried to round Cape Horn against a headgale.  He swore he would do it, and when the gale increased, laughed at the fears of his crew, smoked his pipe and swilled his beer.  As all his efforts were unavailing, he cursed God, and was then condemned to navigate always without putting into port, only having gall to drink and red-hot iron to eat, and eternally to watch.

In Normandy the Phantom Boat puts in at All Souls. The watchman of the wharf sees a vessel come within hail at midnight, and hastens to cast it a line; but at this same moment the boat disappears, and frightful cries are heard that make the hearer shudder, for they are recognised as the voices of sailors shipwrecked that year. Hood has described this in *The Phantom Boat of All Souls' Night*.

The theme has been adopted by novelists, poets, and dramatists. It is a tale told in various forms in nearly every maritime country, and till of late years sailors firmly believed in the existence of the Flying Dutchman, and dreaded seeing the phantom vessel.

These are all the abraded remains of the ancestral belief of our Aryan forefathers relative to the souls of the deceased being conveyed over the river of Vaiterañi, 'hard to cross,' of the Vedas, the Styx of the Greeks, the Gjöll of the Scandinavians, the earth surrounding river, into the land of spirits beyond.[1]

---

[1] The idea that souls 'go out with the tide,' noticed in *David Copperfield*, is connected with the same myth.

# CHAPTER VII

## FETCHES

In the infancy of man there were two phenomena that sorely perplexed him : his reflection in standing water, and his shadow. The universal ignorance of the most element-ary laws of Nature goes far to explain the origin of many myths that were adopted as solutions of problems not understood. Why did a man, on looking into still water, see himself reproduced? He knew nothing of the principle of reflection, and he supposed that he saw a real double of himself. What was the cause of the shadow dogging his steps? It was not caused by his body intercepting the rays of the sun. That was a conception far beyond his reach. He supposed that his shadow was his attendant spirit. Consequently he had two companions—one luminous and the other dark; one good and the other evil.

I had plate-glass windows in my dining-room. Frequently peacocks, seeing them-selves reflected in the panes, flew at them and shattered the glass, supposing that they saw rivals in the affections of the pea-hens. Tigers have been caught by placing mirrors

in traps.  The tiger approaches, sees his
reflection, enters to rub noses or to bite the
beast of his species he sees.  Primitive man
had no greater degree of intelligence in the
particular of his reflection than have peacocks
and tigers.

Throughout the Aryan stock we find a
belief in fetches, wraiths, or doubles, *i.e.* of
man being attended by his duplicate, often
considered as a guardian spirit; in a good
many places we find also a belief in an evil-
minded, mischievous genius as well.  These
are none other than a survival of old conceptions relative to the reflection and the
shadow.

I have known children cry out with rage
when a comrade whipped or stamped on
their shadow, crying out that it hurt them,
or at least was an insult.

The Greeks held that there were *agatho-
dæmones*, good spirits, also *kakodæmones*,
attached to men swaying them to this side
or to the other; and Socrates took counsel
of, and followed the guidance of, his dæmon.
It was not till Christianity occupied the field
that these demons were all comprehended
as devils.

The Romans had their *genii*; every man
had his genius, an attendant spirit; even the

gods were supposed to have their *genii*.
All the acts of life from birth to death, all
the vicissitudes of life and human activities,
all the relations between men and their
fellows, all enterprises, were due to the
impulses afforded by these guardian spirits.
Every household had its Lares and Penates,
but these were of a different order, as they
were ancestral deities, the spirits of the
founders of the family.

To get deeper into the beliefs of an Aryan
people on this topic, we must go to Scandinavian and German sources.

The Norsemen believed that every man
had his *fylgja*, follower, a spirit intimately
related to him, and that died when he did.
It did not always follow—it often preceded
him to look into the future and foretell what
was to be. When the fylgja preceded any
one it was possible to stumble over it. When
a certain Thorsteinn was seven years old,
he came running with childish impetuosity
into the room of one Geitir. In so doing he
tripped and sprawled on the floor, whereat
Geitir laughed. Somewhat later, Thorsteinn
asked what had occasioned this outburst of
merriment; whereupon the other answered :
'I saw, what you did not see, as you burst
into the room, for there followed you a white

bear, running in front of you, but when it saw
me it remained stationary, and you stumbled
over it.' This was Thorsteinn's own fylgja,
and Geitir concluded from its appearance
that the lad was destined to great things.

The fylgja was often seen in animal shape
—an interesting reminiscence of transmigration; for though the belief in the metempsychosis of the human soul had been given
up, the idea lingered on and attached itself to
the companion spirit. The fylgjar showed
themselves sometimes in the form of men,
but also in that of any beast which represented
the character or temperament of the man it
followed. Brave men had their companion
spirits in the shape of bears or wolves. That
of a crafty man appeared as a fox. A timorous
man had a fylgja in the form of a hare or
a small bird.

The Icelander Einarr Eyjólfsson foresaw
the death of his brother Gudmund in dream.
He fancied that an ox with long horns
ascended out of the Eyjafjord and leaped
upon the high seat of Gudmund in his farm
of Madruvöllr, and there fell dead. This ox,
said Einarr, is a man's fylgja. That same
day his brother returned from a journey,
and took his place in the high seat in his
hall, and sank out of it dead.

Njal and Thord went together into a field in which a goat had been seen, which none could drive away. All at once Thord exclaimed, 'This is very strange.' 'What do you see that is strange?' asked Njal. 'I see,' answered Thord, 'the goat lying drenched in blood.' Njal replied, 'That is no goat, it is something else.' 'What is it, then?' asked Thord. 'Look out for yourself,' said Njal; 'you are *fey*, and that is your following spirit.'

The fylgjar come into the world in the caul of a new-born child. If this caul be burnt or thrown away, the man has lost his guardian spirit for his life. In Norway a departing guest is always attended to the door, to make sure that the valve is kept open long enough to allow the spirit to pass out after the man.

In Germany the Companion Spirit is called Jüdel, or Gütel, and when a child laughs in sleep it is said the Jüdel is playing with him. If the guardian spirit keeps the child restless, something is given to it to distract its attention from its little ward.

The idea of the Companion Spirit has been christianised into that of the Guardian Angel. St Bernard says in one of his sermons: 'Whenever you perceive that you are sorely tempted,

and that a great trouble menaces, invoke
your guardian, your teacher, your helper.
In difficulties, in tribulation, in any circumstances, in any hard pressure, have respect to
your angel. Never venture, in his presence,
to do that which you would not do before
me.' Cæsarius of Heisterbach says that to
every man pertains a good, but also a bad
angel. Although the fetch or doppelgänger,
as the Germans call him, has been melted
into the Guardian Angel, he has for all that,
in many cases, retained his identity ; and
stories are not uncommon of his appearance.

Some years ago I was walking through the
cloister at Hurstpierpoint College, when I saw
coming towards me the bursar. I spoke to
him. He turned and looked at me, but passed
on without a word. I went on to the matron's
apartment, and there the identical man was.
I exclaimed : 'Hallo, P., I have just passed
you and spoken to you in the cloister !'
He turned very pale and said, 'I have not
left this room.' 'Well,' said I, 'I could swear
to an alibi any day.'

A Mr Macnish, quoted by Mrs Crowe, tells
the following story : Mr H. was one day
walking along the street, apparently in good
health, when he saw, or supposed he saw, his
acquaintance, Mr C., walking before him.

He called to him aloud, but he did not seem
to hear him, and continued walking on.
Mr H. then quickened his pace for the
purpose of overtaking him, but the other
increased his also, as if to keep ahead of his
pursuer, and proceeded at such a rate that
Mr H. found it impossible to make up to
him. This continued for some time, till,
on Mr C. reaching a gate, he opened it and
passed in, slamming it violently in Mr H.'s
face. Confounded at such treatment from
a friend, the latter instantly opened the gate,
and looked down the long lane into which it
led, where, to his astonishment, no one was
to be seen. Determined to unravel the
mystery, he then went to Mr C.'s house, and
his surprise was great to hear that he was
confined to his bed, and had been so for
several days. A week or two afterwards
these gentlemen met at the house of a mutual
friend, when Mr H. related the circumstances,
jocularly telling Mr C. that, as he had seen
his wraith, he of course could not live long.
The person addressed laughed heartily, as
did the rest of the party; but in a few days
Mr C. was attacked with putrid sore throat,
and died; and within a short period of his
death, Mr H. was also in his grave.

In the biography of John Reinhard

Hedinger, Court chaplain in 1698 to Duke
Eberhard Ludwig of Würtemberg, appears
a curious story.  The duke was a sadly
immoral man, and after Hedinger had
repeatedly urged him to a better life, he
preached in the Court chapel against the sins
to which the duke was most addicted.  The
prince was furious, and sent orders to the
Court chaplain to come to him alone in the
palace at a certain hour.  Hedinger went
and was introduced.  The intention of the
duke was to reprimand him harshly and then
punish him severely.  When the chaplain
entered the cabinet of the prince, the latter
stared at him with astonishment, and said,
'Why have you not come alone?'  'I am
alone, your serene highness.'  'No, you are
not,' retorted the duke, with his eyes fixed
on the right side of the Court preacher.
Hedinger replied gravely: 'But I am—quite
alone.  Your highness, if God has sent His
angel to stand by me, I know nothing about
it.'  The duke dismissed him, showing all the
signs of profound agitation.  Whether this
were an angel, or Hedinger's double, cannot
be said, as Eberhard Ludwig did not give
a description of what he saw.

The musician Glück was staying in Ghent.
While there he was spending an evening

with some friends. He returned to his
lodgings one moonlight evening, when he
observed going before him a figure that
closely resembled himself. It took every
turn through the streets which he was accustomed to take, and finally, on reaching the
door, drew out a key, opened it, and entered.
On this the musician turned round, went
back to his friends, and earnestly entreated
to be taken in for the night. Next morning
they accompanied him to his lodgings, and
found that the heavy wooden beams of the
ceiling of Glück's sleeping-room had fallen
down in the night and crushed the bed. It
was obvious that had he passed the night
there he must have been killed.

Barham, in his *Reminiscences*, relates the
story of a respectable young woman, who was
roused in the night by hearing somebody in
her room, and that on looking up she saw
a young man to whom she was engaged.
Extremely offended at such an intrusion,
she bade him instantly depart if he wished
ever to speak with her again. Whereupon
he told her that he was to die that day six
weeks, and then disappeared. Having ascertained that the youth could not possibly
have been in her room, she was naturally
much alarmed, and her evident depression

leading to some inquiries, she communicated what had occurred to the family with whom she lived. They attached little importance to what seemed so improbable, more especially as the young man continued in perfectly good health, and was entirely ignorant of the prediction, which was carefully kept from him. When the fatal day arrived the girl became cheerful, and as the ladies with whom she lived went on their morning ride, they observed to each other that the prophecy did not seem likely to be fulfilled. On their return, however, they saw her running up the avenue towards the house, in great agitation, and learned that her lover was then either dead or dying.

In Yorkshire the wraith or double is called a waft. There is one night in the year in which the wafts of those who are about to die proceed to the church and may be seen. This is St Mark's Eve, and any one who is curious to know about the death of his fellow-parishioners must keep watch in the church porch on that eve for an hour on each side of midnight for three successive years. Mr Henderson says in his *Northern Folklore* :—

On the third year they will see the forms of those doomed to die within the twelvemonth passing, one

by one, into the church. If the watcher fall asleep
during his vigil he will die himself during the year.
I have heard, however, of one case in which the
intimation was given by the sight of the watcher's
own form and features. It is that of an old woman
at Scarborough, who kept St Mark's vigil in the porch
of St Mary's in that town about eighty years ago.
Figure after figure glided into the church, turning
round to her as they went in, so that she recognised
their familiar faces. At last a figure turned and
gazed at her; she knew herself, screamed, and fell
senseless to the ground. Her neighbours found her
there in the morning, and carried her home, but
she did not long survive the shock.

I knew of a case far more recent, at
Monkokehampton, in North Devon, when a
stalwart young carpenter resolved on keeping
watch. He saw two pass him, and then
his own wraith, that looked hard at him.
He fled and took to his bed. The rector
visited him and did all in his power to con-
vince the man that he had been victim to
hallucination or a dream. The doctor visited
him and could find nothing really the matter
with him. Nevertheless he died within a
fortnight.

## CHAPTER VIII

### SKULLS

IN mediæval churches, castles, and mansions where there is a parapet rising from the wall and obscuring a portion of the roof, this parapet is supported at intervals by corbels, that usually represent heads of either men or beasts, very frequently grotesque. These corbels are not of any great structural importance, though they add to architectural decoration. They are, in fact, a perpetuation of a traditional usage earlier than the construction of buildings of stone. When buildings such as halls were erected of wood, and even later, when the walls were of masonry, the tye beams of the roof projected beyond the supporting walls. These tye beams sustained the principals and the king-post, and rested on the wall-plate. Such was the earliest and simplest form of roof, and it is one that remained in use till Norman times. The stability of the roof depended on the tye beam, which, where it protruded beyond the walls, was sawn off against the grain, and was there most vulnerable, subject to the drive of the weather, and liable to rot. For

its protection skulls were hung upon these
extremities; and when stone buildings came
to be erected with parapets upon them,
then under the string-course that maiked
the wall-plate corbels were added, and the
place of the skulls was supplied by stone
figures representing the heads of men or
beasts. This was not the case only in Gothic
architecture; the same adaptation or modification may be seen in that of Greece and
Rome, where the skull, mainly of an ox,
forms a principal feature in the ornament of
an external cornice, and seems to indicate
that in early days the heads of the victims
sacrificed were thus employed.

Nowadays the sportsman nails up the
skulls and antlers of the stags he has shot,
or the masks of foxes he has hunted, in his
hall; but in Bavaria and Austria they still
decorate the exterior as well as the interior
of the shooting-lodge. There exists naturally
in every sportsman an ambition to bring
home and exhibit some trophy of his exploits;
and as at the present day his energies and
barbarous instincts are confined to the slaying
of wild animals, it is only the heads of wild
animals that he can display to his own satisfaction and that of admiring friends.

But it was otherwise when war was the

great occupation of man and his great enjoy-
ment. Then he preserved the heads of his
enemies killed in fair fight; and after they
had been efficiently dried, he hooked them
on to the ends of the tye beams of his house,
or dangled them inside against his walls,
and was able to yarn to his comrades over
each, and tell all the incidents of the fight,
and display his superior courage or adroit-
ness. Every single head provided a theme
for a story on a winter's evening, and every
head pointed out proved conclusively that
the story was fact and not fiction.

The head-hunting of the Dyak of Borneo
is but a degraded and despicable survival.
A girl will not marry a native till he has some
heads to show. Accordingly he lurks among
the rushes till the girls come down to the
river-side for their ablutions, when he dashes
among them and cuts off as many heads as
he can secure victims. Such trophies are
worthless as evidences of his heroism, but
they pass and are accepted.

'I have cut off four heads' said a Dyak
to his fellow.

'I seven.'

Thus a missionary in Borneo overheard
two natives conversing. And a few weeks
later the second was dead. His village friends

hooked his body out of the river. But it
was now headless. Then they knew, and the
missionary also knew, that now the other
owned five heads.

The reason why only the skulls are preserved is that this is comparatively easy.
The body itself decays and moulders, and is
thus not only difficult to preserve but also
has the repulsive properties of soft corrupting
flesh, whereas it is always easy to keep the
skull. But even that may be felt too
cumbrous, and the North American Indian
contented himself with a scalp as a trophy;
and the ancient Irish chief extracted the
brain of his slain enemy, mixed it with chalk,
rolled it into a ball, and so preserved a trophy
of his prowess.

Jehu had the seventy sons of Ahab beheaded
in Samaria and set up in two heaps at the
entrance of the palace at Jezreel, and I
have seen a photograph of such piles before
the doorway of the Bey of Tunis. The last
exhibition of heads as a decoration was over
Temple Bar, when those of the Jacobite rebels
of 1746 were set up there on iron rods. They
remained there till 1772, when one of them
fell down in a storm, and the others soon
followed. Previous to the Rebellion of 1745,
for about thirty years, Temple Bar exhibited

the head of a barrister named Layer, who
had been executed for a Jacobite conspiracy
soon after Atterbury's plot.

The stone balls that adorn the gateposts
into a manorial park actually, it is believed,
represent heads, and were set up to show that
the lord of that manor possessed right to
pronounce capital sentences. But now they
are on the gateposts of every petty suburban
villa. At Görlitz, north of the Riesen Gebirge,
in the market-place above the town hall,
are iron rods or spikes; half-way up each is
a ball, to represent a head that has fallen
under the sword of the city executioner.
When I was a boy at Pau, in the South of
France, there was a house in the Grande
Place that had been erected by a retired
executioner who had had lively times during
the Reign of Terror. Along the front was
a balustrade for a parapet, and at intervals
stone balls, and these were said to represent
the number of heads that he had cut off
with the guillotine.

Although among the Aryans human sacrifice was not uncommon, I do not find any
evidence that the heads of the victims were
made use of as ornaments. This was a
privilege reserved for warriors who had
fallen in battle. Nor were slaves decapitated

for this purpose, though very frequently sacrificed.

It is, however, other in Africa. In certain tribes a man's dignity depends on the number of heads of slaves he has had decapitated and which he can show.

In the North-West Congo, a rich man of the Babangi tribe endeavours to send forward a number of his attendants as out-runners to provide comfortable quarters for himself and to minister to his convenience when he arrives. He calls together all his attendants to a great feast of palm-wine and fish. But eating and drinking are only the preliminaries to the real business that has to be transacted— the sacrifice of a slave. The actual victim is not announced beforehand, the essential reason being that he has to be taken out of the midst of the revellers and then and there consigned to death.

Before the residences of well-to-do Babangi are tables laden with skulls, some blanched, others still with the skin about them and in a condition of putrefaction. The black gentleman conducts his admiring and envious guest about the table and points out to him what a large retinue he will possess in the other world. He fully understands that, when he is dead, his legal successors will

grudge sending human victims after him.
Their view rather is : 'Why should we send
slaves to the man in the other world, when we
ourselves shall want them to provide for our
comfort hereafter?'

The custom among the Scandinavians and
others of the Aryan race of drinking out of
skulls of their enemies is but another instance
of disregard of the human frame, a purposeful
exhibition of contempt for the skull.

The earliest instance is in the Eddaic lay of
Viglund or Veluni, the same as the English
Wayland the Smith.   That the story was
familiar to our Anglo-Saxon forefathers we
know, because Alfred the Great refers to it.
It was also well known in Germany.

Viglund was a smith who lived by the side
of a lake in the realms of Niduth, King of
Sweden.   Hearing of his great skill, Niduth
and his men visit the hut whilst the smith is
absent, and find a number of gold rings strung
together.   They take one.   On Viglund's
return he finds that one is missing ; nevertheless he goes to sleep, but on waking he is
surrounded and taken prisoner.   The queen,
mistrusting the man, has him hamstrung.
The king sets him on an island in a lake, and
bids him make gold and silver ornaments
for him and fashion steel weapons.   Niduth

had two sons, whom he strictly forbade going
near the forge. They were, however, inquisi-
tive, and did visit it, and persuaded Viglund
to show them what he had made. Viglund
dazzled their eyes with his work, and promised
to give them of it if on the following day
they would return with the utmost secrecy.
They agreed and went, whereupon Viglund
murdered them both, sunk their bodies in
a morass, but chased their skulls in silver
and formed out of them two drinking-bowls
for the king. He set the boys' eyes in gold
and sent them to the queen as brooches, and
the teeth of her brothers he made into a necklace for their sister. The story is extremely
barbarous, and, as it can be traced even to
Greece, it probably forms part of a legend
told prior to the Aryan dispersion. The
necklace of teeth is a specially early trait.

Should love and devotion, and the effort
to maintain relations with the departed,
triumph over fear, then the reverse process
to the getting rid of the dead ensued. The
dead were preserved at least in part. As,
however, the children of Nature are always
wavering between fear and respect for the
dead, so also all burial rites oscillate between
the destruction and the preservation of the
body. Thus it happens that extremely

opposite sentiments give rise to most com-
plicated practices and conceptions, which
are frequently in flagrant contradiction with
one another.

Be that as it may.  I think that what we
shall see in Europe of inconsistencies is due
to there having been in it the Aryan race,
which placed little value on the body, but
esteemed the soul as the essential quality of
personality; and on the other hand, the
Rude-Stone-Monument Builders, who had no
conception of the soul as apart from the
body, and whose religion consisted not in
animism at all, but in ancestor worship,
this is to say, of the ancestor buried in his
cairn or dolmen.

We know that periodically a family or
tribe opened the ancestral tomb and scraped
and cleaned the bodies of their forebears.
We know this, because we can trace the
scratches made on their bones with flint
scrapers, as also, because not having a perfect
knowledge of anatomy, they sometimes replaced the bones wrongly, as the tibia of the
right leg placed on the left side.  We know
also, from actual finds, that a loving widow
would occasionally secure the skull of the
late lamented and suspend it round her neck;
or if not the entire skull, yet a portion of it,

prized as an inestimable treasure, as it kept her in some relation with him whom she had lost.

It is remarkable how completely the Roman Church has surrendered to the usages of the primeval man in the cult of relics. I have seen repeatedly above altars in Switzerland and Tyrol grinning skulls under glass forming the most conspicuous object of adoration above an altar. The builder of megalithic monuments has passed away, or been absorbed by nobler and more intelligent peoples, but his worship of the dead remains intact ; the only difference being that the devotion is no longer offered to the skull of an ancestor, but to that of a more or less fictitious saint. I suppose that the officials are in some places becoming a little ashamed of this, for at St Ursula's, Cologne, where a few years ago the space above the arches and below the clerestory windows was crowded with small boxes containing skulls, they have of late years been placed under curtains. But the sacristy still maintains the appearance of a charnel-house.

It is significant how the cult of images and relics disappeared out of England and Scotland without leaving a trace, or only the faintest.

At Llandeilo, under the Presilly Hills, in
South Wales, is a holy well of St Teilo;
and in the farm-house hard by, Mr Melchior,
the tenant, preserves the brain-pan of the
skull that was shown and used before the
Reformation as that of the saint.  He is the
hereditary guardian of the relic.  Unhappily
for its genuineness, the open sutures prove
that it must have been the head of a young
person, and as Teilo died at an advanced age,
it could not have belonged to him.  Moreover, a part of the superciliary ridge remains,
and this is of slight elevation, so that it
seems almost certain to have been a portion
of a young woman's head.  Patients drank
water till quite recently from the well out
of the reputed skull, and many cures are
recorded.

At Skalholt, in Iceland, was preserved and
venerated the supposed skull of St Thorlac,
till on examination it proved to be a cocoa-
nut that had been washed up in one of the
fjords.

But if there remain but the most meagre
trace of the worship of saintly relics in
England, there remain tokens of what appears
to have been at a remote period a veneration
for the heads of ancestors or founders of
houses.

Near Launceston is the ancient house of Tresmarrow that belonged to Sir Hugh Piper, Governor of Launceston Castle under Charles I. By the marriage of Philippa, daughter and heiress of Sir Hugh, the house and property passed into the Vyvyan family; then it passed to a Dr Luke, whose wife was a Miss Vyvyan. He sold it to an old yeoman farmer of the name of Dawe, and it remained in the Dawe family till about five years ago, when it was again sold.

Now, in a niche in the old buildings for centuries was to be seen a human skull. All recollection of whose it was had passed away. One of the Dawes, disliking its presence, had it buried, but thereupon ensued such an uproar, such mighty disturbances, that it was on the morrow dug up again and replaced in its recess. The Dawe family, when they sold Tresmarrow, migrated to Canada, and have taken the skull with them.

There was a 'screaming skull' at Waddon, in Dorsetshire, about fifty years ago, kept respectfully in a recess on the stairs; but as it was liable to be fractious and cause disturbances in the house, it was given to the Dorchester Museum, where it now is. The story about it is that it was the head of a negro, and it bore on it the mark of

a cut from a sword.  The black man went
to his master's room at night, and the latter,
believing him to be a burglar, killed him
by mistake.  He was killed in the bedroom
over the dining-room.  The owners of Waddon
were the Grove family of Zeals, in Wiltshire.
When Miss Chafyn Grove died some years
ago, her cousin, Mr Troyte Bullock, inherited,
but with the property had to take the name
of Chafyn Grove.

A few miles distant from Waddon is
Bettiscombe.  Here also is a 'screaming skull.'
The house was rebuilt in Queen Anne's reign,
but the richly carved wainscoting and fine
old oak stairs pertain to the earlier house
that was pulled down when the present
mansion was built.  This was done by Azariah
Pinney, who had joined Monmouth's forces,
and was exiled to the West Indies, he being
one of those who escaped sentence of death
by Judge Jeffreys at the 'Bloody Assizes,'
held at Dorchester, after the Rebellion.  His
life was spared through the influence of
a friend at the Court of James II.  He
remained in the West Indies for a period of
ten years, and then returned with a black
servant, to whom he was much attached;
and then the man died; but whether the
skull be his, or, if so, why it was preserved

above ground, none can say. It would seem
probable, however, that it was taken along
with the wainscoting out of the earlier house.

The prevailing superstition is that, if it
be brought out of the house, the house itself
will rock to its foundations, and the person
guilty of the sacrilegious act will die within
the year. The house had remained unin-
habited for some years until, about 1760 or
1770, a farmer came into occupation. Finding
the skull, he declared with an oath that he
would not have the thing there, and he had
it thrown into a pool of water. During that
night and the next the farmer heard some
uncanny noises, and on the third day he said
he would have the skull back. He did so, and
then, as the story goes, all the noises ceased.
It has been carefully preserved since, and kept
in a kind of loft under the roof in a cigar box.

In Looe Island, off East and West Looe,
is still, or was a few years ago, a skull preserved in a cupboard in the sitting-room,
behind glass. I have not been able to find
any tradition connected with it. Looe Island
was at one time a great resort of smugglers,
till a coastguard station was established on it.

At Warbleton Priory, near Heathfield, in
Sussex, were two skulls preserved till some
few years ago, when they were stolen, greatly

to the wrath of the proprietor. Legends were told, in the usual way, of the hideous cries and wailing that would ensue were they disturbed. But there has been no trouble in the house since. Very vague traditions remain as to their origin.

Near Chapel-en-le-Frith, in Derbyshire, is a farm-house where the skull of one called 'Dickie' is preserved. A skull in perfect preservation is at Higher Chilton Farm, in the village of Chilton Cantelo, Somerset. This is the headpiece of one Theophilus Brome, who died in 1670, and was buried in the north transept of the church. Collinson, in his *History of Somerset*, referring to Chilton Cantelo and Brome, says :—

There is a tradition in this parish that the person here interred requested that his head might be taken off before his burial and be preserved at the farm-house near the church, where a head—chop-fallen enough—is still shown, which the tenants of the house have often endeavoured to commit to the bowels of the earth, but have as often been deterred by horrid noises portentive of sad displeasure; and about twenty years since (which was perhaps the last attempt) the sexton, in digging the place for the skull's repository, broke the spade in two pieces, and uttered a solemn asseveration never more to attempt an act so evidently repugnant to the quiet of Brome's Head.

The truth of the story that the skull pre-served in the house is that of Theophilus

Brome was proved during the restoration of
the church, some forty-five or fifty years ago,
when Brome's tomb was opened and the
skeleton discovered *minus* the head.

Now, we may ask, Why did Brome desire
his head to be kept in the house? He was
assuredly possessed with a traditional idea
that it would be good for him, or for the
household rather, to have his head as its
guardian and overlooker of the household.
Thus the head of Bran the Blessed was
taken to London and buried where now stands
the Tower; and it was foretold that so long
as it remained there no invasion could be
made of Britain. In a fit of vainglorious
temerity King Arthur dug it up, saying
that he chose not to hold the island except
by his own prowess; and I have heard of
a Black Forest farmer who desired to be
buried on a hill commanding his whole land,
so that he might see to it that the labourers
did their work properly.[1]

Ivar the Boneless, King of Northumbria,
when dying, ordered his body to be planted
in a great mound, where he might watch and
protect the confines of the kingdom, and he
declared that Northumbria would not be

[1] Precisely the same thing occurs in an Icelandic
saga.

subdued so long as he remained therein.
It was said that one reason why King Harald
Hardrede fell in the battle of Stamford
Bridge was that Ivar the Boneless was engaged
against him. It was further said, later, that
William the Bastard, when he proceeded
north to quell the turbulent spirit of the
Northumbrians, disinterred the incorrupt
body of Ivar, had a mighty pile of wood
collected, and burned the carcass to ashes,
after which he set to work in most ruthless
fashion to devastate Northumbria.

In Wardley Hall, Lancashire, is preserved
the skull of Father Ambrose, that is to say,
Alexander Barlow, one of the Papist martyrs.
For saying Mass on Sunday, April 25, 1641,
he was seized by an infuriated mob, led by
a Puritan minister, and was hanged, drawn,
and quartered on September 10. His head
was impaled on the tower of the old church,
Manchester, but was afterwards removed
and taken to Wardley Hall, where the skull
is likely to remain in its accustomed place
so long as Wardley Hall stands, for a
clause is always inserted in leases of the house
forbidding its removal. Some years ago,
when the old house was let out in tenements
to colliers, an attempt was made to get rid
of it, but it was said that no peace ensued in

the house till it was restored. Once it was flung into the moat, which had to be drained to recover it.

And now I come to a case that, if I mistake not, lets in light on the subject of these screaming skulls, and explains the reason why they exist.

Burton Agnes is situated in the East Riding of Yorkshire, and the hall is a noble structure. The estate, which was anciently owned by the De Somervilles, passed in the reign of Edward I. to the Griffith family, which died out in three co-heiresses, sisters, in the last years of Queen Elizabeth. As they were very wealthy, they resolved on rebuilding the family mansion in the style of the period, and the youngest sister, Anne, took the keenest interest in planning and furnishing the hall. When it was complete, the ladies took up their abode in it; but one day soon after, Anne was murdered on her way to visit some friends by ruffians, then called wood-rangers, for her purse and rings. She had been stunned by them by a blow over the head with a cudgel, and was carried back to Burton Agnes; but although she lingered during five days, she never recovered, and finally died. In her last conscious intervals she besought her sisters, when she was dead, to sever her head from her body and preserve it in the house that had been her delight and pride.

The two surviving Misses Griffith thought this an absurd request, and did not comply with it. But the noises in the house, of things falling, of doors slamming, cries and moans, so scared them that they had the family vault opened, the head of sister Anne detached and installed in the hall, whereupon the noises ceased.

The Boyntons of Barmston inherited Burton Agnes by right of descent from Sir Matthew Boynton, who married the last surviving of the three sisters, and was created a baronet in 1618. The Boyntons had the skull buried in the garden; but no luck attended the house and family till it was returned to its accustomed place.

Now, here we have the foundress and fashioner of the house, at her particular desire, requiring her skull to be for ever preserved in it; undoubtedly like that of Brân, who watched for the interests of Britain. When Brân had been wounded in the foot by a poisoned arrow in Ireland, he bade the seven survivors of his party cut off his head and take it back with them to Wales. He told them that they would sit long at dinner at Harlech, where the head would converse with them and be as entertaining as it had ever been when attached to the trunk. From Harlech they were to proceed to Gresholm, and remain there feasting in company with the head so long as they did not open a door that looked towards Cornwall. Should they open that door, then they must set out for London, and there, on the White Hill, bury it with its face towards France; so long as the head remained undisturbed in this position, the island would have nothing to fear from foreign invasion.

There is an Irish story also concerning a speaking head. Finn had his hunting-lodge in Jeffia. Whilst he was absent, his fool Lomna discovered Finn's wife engaged in an intrigue with one Cairbre, and he divulged the fact to Finn. Next time that Finn was abroad, Cairbre returned to see the lady, and, discovering who had betrayed what he had done, cut off Lomna's head and carried it away with him. Finn, in the evening, found a headless body in the booth, and at once concluded that this was Lomna's, and that Cairbre had been his murderer. He went in pursuit, and tracked Cairbre and his party to an empty house, where they had been cooking fish on a stone, with Lomna's head on

a spike by the fire.    The first portion cooked
was evenly divided by Cairbre among his
followers; but not a morsel was put within
the lips of the head, which thereupon chanted
an obscure verse of remonstrance.    The
second charge cooked was distributed in the
same manner, and again the head sang
a verse expressive of indignation.    Cairbre
then said, 'Put the head outside; it has but
evil words for us.'    No sooner had the order
been obeyed than the head outside sang a
third verse, and Finn and his party arrived
on the spot.

In Scandinavian mythology Odin had the
head of Mimir, that had been cut off, ever
by him as guide and adviser.

In the *Arabian Nights* is the story of the
Greek king and the physician whom he has condemned to decapitation.    The latter gives the
king a book, and bids him question his head
as to what he wants to know after it has
been cut off, and it will answer him.    In the
mediæval story of Friar Bacon, it is a brazen
head that the friar and Bungey fashion,
and which is to instruct them how to wall
England round with brass.    Through the
dullness of the man Miles set to watch it, the
favourable moment is lost.

That at some time in the remote past the

skull of the ancestor was regarded as oracular
is possible enough, but we have no evidence
to that effect. What we have seen has been
the survival of the preservation of the skull,
presumedly of an ancestor, at all events of
a founder, as a protecting relic, not genius,
for no thought of spirit enters into it. It is
the osseous mass of bone that is the guardian,
not any soul that once inhabited it.

I may instance the usages of the natives of
the Torres Straits. Here the corpse is first
laid upon a horizontal frame sustained by
posts at the corners. The moisture is pressed
out, and then after a long time, when the
bone is everywhere exposed, the head is
detached, and the rest buried or thrown into
the sea, after which some funeral feasts
ensue. The important part of the ceremony
consists in the solemn delivery of the skull
to the survivors. Sometimes the head is
placed at night on the old bed of the deceased,
so that he seems to be sleeping with the
family as in his lifetime, till at last the head
of the family, or the chief, puts the skull
as a pillow under his own head. Thenceforth it is treated with great respect and is
given a sort of hutch in which to rest. One
such from the Solomon Islands may be seen
in the British Museum.

The few 'screaming skulls' in the country
may be regarded as the last lingering remains
of a custom once general, at a still earlier
date universal.    But it is a custom that goes
back into the darkest ages of mankind—at
all events, to that of the Dolmen Builders,
who used stone weapons, and had not as
yet acquired the knowledge of bronze.

## CHAPTER IX

### PIXIES AND BROWNIES

In the year 1838, when I was a small boy
of four years old, we were driving to Mont-
pellier, on a hot summer day, over the long
straight road that traverses a pebble and
rubble strewn plain on which grows nothing
save a few aromatic herbs.

I was sitting on the box with my father,
when to my great surprise I saw legions of
dwarfs of about two feet high running along
beside the horses—some sat laughing on the
pole, some were scrambling up the harness
to get on the backs of the horses.    I remarked
to my father what I saw, when he abruptly
stopped the carriage and put me inside beside
my mother, where, the conveyance being

closed, I was out of the sun. The effect was
that little by little the host of imps diminished
in number till they disappeared altogether.
When my wife was a girl of fifteen, she was
walking down a lane in Yorkshire between
green hedges, when she saw, seated in one
of the privet hedges a little green man,
perfectly well made, who looked at her with
his beady black eyes. He was about a foot
or eighteen inches high. She was so frightened
that she ran home. She cannot recall exactly
in what month this took place, but knows
that it was a summer day.

One day a son of mine, a lad of about
twelve, was sent into the garden to pick
pea-pods for the cook to shell for dinner.
Presently he rushed into the house as white
as chalk, to say that whilst he was engaged
upon the task imposed upon him he saw
standing between the rows of peas a little
man wearing a red cap, a green jacket, and
brown knee-breeches, whose face was old
and wan, and who had a gray beard and
eyes as black and hard as sloes. He stared
so intently at the boy that the latter took to
his heels. I know exactly when this occurred,
as I entered it in my diary, and I know when
I saw the imps by looking into my father's
diary, and though he did not enter the

circumstance, I recall the vision to-day as distinctly as when I was a child.

Now, in all three cases, these apparitions were due to the effect of a hot sun on the head. But such an explanation is not sufficient. Why did all three see small beings of a very similar character? With pressure on the brain and temporary hallucination the pictures presented to the eye are never originally conceived, they are reproductions of representations either seen previously or conceived from descriptions given by others.

In my case and that of my wife, we saw imps, because our nurses had told us of them and their freaks. In the case of my son, he had read *Grimm's Tales* and seen the illustrations to them.

Both St Hildegarde and St Bridget of Sweden had visions that were supposed to fill gaps in the Gospel narrative or amplify the stories there told. It is noticeable that in these revelations there is not a waft of Orientalism, they are vulgarly Occidental. Every one may be explained by the paintings, carvings, and miniatures with which these ladies had been familiar from childhood. If we had not these monuments of mediæval art remaining, we could reconstruct Catholic iconography from the revelations of these ecstatics.

We may now go a step farther back. Where did our nurses, whence did Grimm obtain their tales of kobolds, gnomes, dwarfs, pixies, brownies, etc.? They derived them from traditions of the past, handed down from generation to generation.

But to go to the root of the matter. In what did the prevailing belief in the existence of these small people originate? I do not myself hold that a widely extended belief, curiously coinciding, whether found in Scandinavia, in Germany, in England, Scotland, and Ireland, can have sprung out of nothing. Everything comes out of an egg or a seed. And I suspect that there did exist a small people, not so small as these imps are represented, but comparatively small beside the Aryans who lived in all those countries in which the tradition of their existence lingers on. They were not, I take it, the Dolmen builders—these are supposed to have been giants because of the gigantic character of their structures. They were a people who did not build at all. They lived in caves, or, if in the open, in huts made by bending branches over and covering them with sods of turf. Consequently in folk-tales they are always represented as either emerging from caverns or from under mounds.

Such slightly constructed residences—much like those of the Lapps—would disappear completely after desertion.

This Little People are represented in folk-lore as peevish and unreliable; often as good humoured, at other times as vindictive.

The Norse, Anglo-Saxon, and German names for them are Alf, Elf, Alb, Ell. In mediæval poems in German the Will-o'-the-Wisp is called Elbisch Feuer, the Elfish fire. We find among the Anglo-Saxons both men's names and also place names that show that this race was then known and respected. Elfric is the Power of the Elf, and is the same as Alfric. Alfred is the Peace of the Alf. We have places such as Ellmoor, Eildon, Elphinstone, Alphington is the tun of a family that did not disdain to claim descent from the Alfs. Elton is the tun of the Elf, and Allerton the residence of a colony of them.[1]    Elberish is the Gnome king in the Nibelungenlied, the Auberon of French legend, the Oberon of the romancers. In Germany, the Elle king has been turned into Erle king by Goethe.

The earliest and purest account of the Elves is obtained from the Icelandic Edda

[1] Among the Harleian MS. is an Anglo-Saxon charm by means of which protection is obtained against elf-shots (ylfa gescot).

and Sagas.   An Alvismal or poem of the
Elf has been preserved from pagan times.
It is true that the small people never pene-
trated to Iceland, but the Icelanders brought
away with them to Iceland the traditions,
songs, stories, and superstitions of Norway,
from which they emigrated.

According to the testimony of several
sagas, there dwelt in Sweden, in remote
times, a gigantic, wild race called Jotuns;
but when the Scandinavians arrived there
arose between them and the Jotuns a war
that lasted for many centuries.   At last these
were driven into the forests and mountains,
and away to the frozen north about the
Gulf of Finland, which thenceforth was
called Jotunheim.   These, I can hardly
doubt, were the builders of the rude stone
monuments in the south of Sweden, in Denmark, and in Jutland that possibly still
retains their name.

But there was a distinct species of Mountain Trolls, or Dwarfs.   These were good
mechanics and cunning, their wives and
daughters were often beautiful.   'This Dwarf
race,' Mr Thorpe thinks, 'seems to spring
from a people that had migrated from the
Eastern countries at a later period, as they
were acquainted with names which they

used in sorcery, accompanied by the harp.
A similar art of enchanting and bewitching
the Laplanders are supposed to possess even
to the present day, and with some probability
it may be conjectured that the Asiatic people,
who in the sagas are mentioned under the
name of Dwarfs, was no other than an immi-
gration of Oriental Lapps, and the origin of
the race among us which still bears that
name.'

The Scandinavians distinguished between
the Light Elves and the Black Elves or
Dwarfs. The former lived in mounds and
the latter in caves; but in all probability
the distinction existed not in blood, but
in mode of habitations. Just as to this day
there are the shore Lapps and the mountain
Lapps.

Popular fancy has idealised the Light Elves
into merry beings that dance their ringlets
on the grass, and because their original habitations have collapsed altogether they have
transferred them to the tumuli of the incinerated dead. But with these latter they
had nothing to do. The barrow is a substitute
for the turf-covered hovel that perished
without leaving a trace.

There is one difficulty in identifying the
Elves and Dwarfs with the Lapps, and that

is the fact that the Dwarfs are regarded, and
have been regarded, as accomplished metal
workers, especially sword-smiths, whereas no
such an art exists among the Lapps of to-day.
It is, however, possible enough that a migration
into Europe of iron-working Lapps may have
taken place, just as the Gipsies came in and
engrossed at one time the trade of pottery
and of tinware makers. And what is abundantly clear from the sagas is that the Norsemen were not accomplished smiths. Their
swords blunted directly or broke; and they
were fain to apply to the Dwarfs to supply
them with finely-tempered blades. How to
temper them in oil the Norsemen knew not.
If they could not get a sword from a Dwarf
they dug into the mounds of dead heroes to
obtain blades they were themselves incom-
petent to manufacture. One would suppose
that such weapons cannot have been very
serviceable corroded as they would be by rust.
All the notable swords were of elfin or dwarf
make—such were Mimung, Excalibur, Duran-
dal, Nagelring, and the famous Tyrfing.
The story of this latter may here be told
in brief. It is contained in one of the finest
and wildest of the sagas. Svafurlami, second
in descent from Odin, King of Gardarik
(Russia), was out hunting one day, but

could find no game. When the sun set, he was in the depths of the forest and knew not his way out. Then he observed two Dwarfs standing before a hill. He drew his sword and dashed in between them and their abode. They pleaded to be allowed to escape, but he asked of them their names, and they replied that the one was named Dyrin and the other Dvallin. Then he knew that they were the most skilful of all workers in iron, that a sword fashioned by them would never rust; it would cut through iron, and secure to him who wielded it certain victory. He granted them their lives on condition that they fabricated for him such a blade.

On the appointed day Svafurlami returned; the Dwarfs came forward and presented him with the sword. As Dvalin stood in the door he said : 'This sword will cause the death of a man every time that it is drawn. Three of the most infamous acts will be done by it, and it will bring about your own ruin.' At that Svafurlami smote at the dwarf, and the blade cut into the hard rock. But the sword was his; he named it Tyrfing, bore it in every battle, and with it slew the giant Thiassi and took his daughter to wife, and had by her a daughter Eyvör.

One day he was engaged in conflict with

the Berserk [1] Arngrim, who bore a shield lined
with plates of steel.  Svafurlami with Tyrfing
smote through it, but with the force of the
blow the blade entered the soil; as he stooped
to withdraw it, Arngrim dexterously twisted
it, and with it clove the king from head to
foot.  Then he carried off Eyvör and married
her.  By Eyvör he became the father of
twelve sons, the eldest named Angantyr,
the fourth Hjörvard.  To Angantyr was
given the sword Tyrfing.  Now, it was customary at Yule for champions to take oath
what they would achieve in the coming year,
and Hjörvard swore that he would win
Ingjbord, daughter of Yngvi, King of Sweden.
Accordingly all the brothers went to Upsala
and demanded the king's daughter for
Hjörvard.  To this objected Hjaltmar, a
champion of Yngvi, and it was decided that
at a given date the brothers should meet
Hjaltmar and his companion, Odd, on the
lone island of Samsey, and decide by battle
who should win the maid.  Before the
appointed day the brothers visited a friendly
Earl Bjartmar, where Angantyr celebrated
his wedding with the earl's daughter.  The

[1] Berserks were men possessed with temporary murder-
ous madness.  Observe in the story that the king finds
a suitable wife in the giant's daughter.   This seems to
show that the Jotuns were not necessarily of gigantic size.

fight took place, all the brothers and Hjaltmar were slain, and Odd buried the sons of Svafurlami along with their weapons in a great mound.  Angantyr left an only child, a daughter named Hervör, who dressed herself as a man, went on Viking expeditions, and visited the island of Samsey with full purpose to recover the sword Tyrfing, that was buried with her father.  A weird account is given of how at night she sought the grave-mound and sang strophes to her father, demanding the surrender of the Dwarfs' blade.  To this, from his grave, Angantyr replies and objects to be parted from it.  But finally the daughter prevails.  The grave-mound gapes, and from amidst lambent flames the sword is flung towards her.  Having obtained possession of Tyrfing, she went to the Court of King Gudmund, where one day she had laid aside the scabbard with Tyrfing in it, whilst playing dice with the king. A retainer of Gudmund ventured to draw the sword and obtain command of it, whereupon Hervör sprang up, seized the blade, and cut the man down.  Eventually Hervör resumed her female habit and married the son of Gudmund, by whom she had two sons, Angantyr and Heidrek.  The elder was peace-loving and amiable, but the younger was malevolent and quarrelsome, and became so intolerable at home that his father banished him. On leaving, his mother handed to him Tyrfing. As he left, his brother Angantyr accompanied him part way. Heidrek drew the sword to admire it, when, as the sun flashed on the blade, the Berserk rage came on him and he cut down his brother. Heidrek went on, joined the Vikings, and as he served King Harald many a good turn he was given in marriage the king's daughter Helga. The destiny of Tyrfing must be fulfilled, and with it Harald fell by the sword under the hand of his son-in-law. Later, Heidrek went to Russia, where he took the king's son in charge as his foster-child. One day when out hunting together the pair were parted from their retinue, when a wild boar appeared. Heidrek's spear broke against the tusks of the beast, whereupon he drew his sword and killed it. But Tyrfing could only be satiated with human blood. Heidrek turned round, but seeing no other man present save his foster-son, slew him. Finally, he was himself transfixed with Tyrfing by his slaves, when he was asleep, and had suspended the fateful weapon over his bed. His son and successor, Angantyr, slew the murderers and recovered the sword. In a battle against the Huns, in which Angantyr was engaged, it committed great execution, but among the slain Angantyr found his own brother Hlodr. Thus ends the story of the Dwarf-fabricated sword Tyrfing.

The introduction of iron into Europe came comparatively late, far earlier in some parts than in others. Even among the Hebrews bronze was much more familiar as a metal than iron. In the four first books of Moses bronze is mentioned eighty-three times, and iron only four times. India is rich in iron ore, but in its early literature iron is only certainly mentioned at the close of the Vaidic period, and then it is called 'dark-blue copper,' the contrary to the South African Kafirs, who call copper 'red' iron, gold 'yellow,' and silver 'white' iron.

In the midst of the sixth century before our era, the work of the blacksmith was strange and excited great curiosity. Herodotus tells a story of a Spartiot who went to Jegæa, in Arcadia, and saw a smith at work, for the first time, with the utmost amazement. There were, in fact, no beds of iron ore in Greece, and all iron was brought to it from the East. The most famous and unsurpassed ironworkers who produced steel weapons were the Chalybii of the Caucasus, sometimes placed in the north of the range, sometimes to the south, but always close to the Black Sea. Their fame was spread through all the ancient world, and to the present day it is stated there is a Caucasian tribe that devotes itself to iron work and supplies the other tribes with weapons.

In the *Seven against Thebes* of Æschylus, the brothers were slain 'with the hammer-wrought Scythian steel.'

Into Italy the use of iron arrived earlier than into Greece, and the Ligurians in the north-west of the peninsula were supposed to be of Greek origin, because that even in historic times they employed bronze lance-heads.

Among the northern inhabitants of Europe it was a much longer time before they became acquainted with iron. Tacitus informs us how rare it was among the Germans in his time (A.D. 100), and Cæsar, when he set foot in Britain, found the island well peopled, with abundance of cattle, and instead of coins using bits of bronze or iron of various weights. In the interior of the land tin was found, and iron, but in small quantities, on the coast. The Britons had no knowledge of alloying copper with tin, consequently all the bronze they had in use was imported.

It would seem from this that as yet the Britons knew nothing of the making of steel, or using iron in any other way than as a currency.

It was even worse in the north-east of Europe. The Esthonians, a Lettish-Prussian people, for hundreds of years of our present reckoning used iron as a rarity, and as weapons employed wooden clubs. The Finns at the same time pointed their spears and arrows with bone 'through deficiency of iron,' as Tacitus says.

A curious story is told us by the Byzantine historian Simocatta. When the Emperor Maurice, in A.D. 591, was marching against the Avars on the shores of the Sea of Marmora, there were brought to him two unarmed men of strange aspect, who carried musical instruments like lutes. It was ascertained from them that the Khan of the Avars had sent to their people, who lived on the coast of the Baltic, demanding aid against the Byzantine Emperor, and they were sent as messengers to reply that they were a peaceable people, unaccustomed to wars, and unacquainted with the use of iron.

That the Gauls and Celts, at least on the Continent, were acquainted with steel weapons is certain from the Hallstadt and La Tène finds. The former may safely be said to derive from an Eastern Asiatic source, probably from the Chalybii of the Caucasus. The La Tène find may, however, be due to indigenous Celtic industry, inspired from the same source.

The importers of Caucasian steel into Europe were the Thracians, who with the Illyrians of the same race occupied the northern part of the Balkan peninsula from the Bosphorus to the Adriatic. Imports across the Bosphorus from Pontus would be numerous, and Thracians and Illyrians would be the distributers along the upper course of the Danube. These primitive people have been expelled from their lands, and driven West by successive waves of invaders from the North, the Goths, the Avars, and the Sclaves; and by pressure from the South by the Macedonian conquerors and the Greek colonists. But they have left their tombs, and these are rich in iron. Bronze was largely in use still, but mainly in ornaments. At Glusinac, in Bosnia, on the eastern slope of the Romanja-Plantina, is a plateau on which are thousands of the graves of these ancient people. They consist of small cairns and cover interments of bodies unburnt, with swords, spear-heads, and axes, ornaments of bronze, beads of glass and amber, tools, knives, pincers, etc., of iron, and hones.

The last remains of the ancient Thracians are the Albanians. They were a small, dark race, probably of Aryan stock, as they so readily assimilated Greek culture. The extensive finds at Hallstadt in the Salzkammergut pertain to the earliest iron age, when that metal was coming into use, but had not as yet supplanted the bronze. The graves at Hallstadt contained skeletons outstretched, others burnt, in the proportion of 525 skeleton graves to 455 containing the ashes of the dead. The remains were of men of moderate size, dolichocephalous, somewhat prognathous, with retreating foreheads; the type is not that of the present inhabitants of this portion of the Alps.

Although in the Icelandic Sagas Sigmund, the Siegfried of the Nibelungenlied, fashions his own sword, it is at the teaching of the Elf; and the Scandinavians never appear to have been expert smiths. They left the fabrication of swords to the Dwarfs. Nor do we ever hear of them as engaged in mining; but the Dwarfs are represented so frequently as standing at the mouth of a cave, or as facing into one, that we may expect that they were miners as well as armourers.

The makers of weapons had their trade
secrets.   From the Wilkina Saga we learn
that Welent, who is none other than Velund,
was set to fabricate a sword for King Nidung.
For this purpose he mixed raspings of iron
with meal, which he made into a paste,
wherewith he fed the geese.   He then collected all their droppings and fashioned the
blade out of that, and it was so wondrous
sharp that it cut through a yard-long flock
of wool that was thrown into a stream and
carried against the edge.   The Egyptians used
to make steel out of meteoric iron by heating
it in a fire made of camels' dung.     The
armourers of Bagdad took iron filings, mixed
it with the food of geese, and from their
excrement formed the celebrated Damascus
blades.   The secret must have been brought
from the East by the first smiths who wandered into Northern Europe.

The Dwarfs and Elves may not have been
all of the same stock.   What is abundantly
evident is that the fabrication of iron was
not of native growth in Northern and Eastern
Europe, it was an importation, and if imported,
it must have been so by a people which was
familiar with the processes, through the
experience of generations.   These may have
come from the Caucasus, and Lapps may

have acquired from them the new art.    Of
that we know nothing.    But I think we do
know enough to say that there did exist, in
England and generally in the British Isles,
in Scandinavia and in Germany, a black-
smithying people, not of Ibernian nor of
Aryan blood, not found in large numbers nor
forming big colonies, but vagrant and dispersed as are the gipsies of the present day.
And I suspect that it is this people who have
occasioned the stories told of pixies, kobolds,
brownies, elves, etc.    Such a people, shy, living
a different life from those for whom they
worked, were sure to excite imagination and
give rise to fantastic stories.    They were
feared as well as respected.    They do not
seem ever to have been ill-treated; they were
too valuable to be molested.    Indeed, as
already instanced, they entered occasionally
into marriage relations with the settled
inhabitants.    The family of Alversleben, in
the north of Germany, takes its name from
an ancestor who spent much of his time with
the elves under a green mound.

But if there were workers in iron and
makers of steel blades, there must have been
also miners, who not only used such iron as
was found in sand and morass, but who
tracked it in veins in the rock.    I do not think

that we have much evidence that the Aryans did this.   But such as the Chalibii, acquainted with iron in all its conditions, would become miners.   And tradition throughout Northern Europe indicates that these were the Dwarfs. In Germany, in Cornwall, and Devon existed, and to some extent exists to this day, the belief that there are Trolls, little old men who work in mines, who are occasionally seen by the miners, but are more often heard by them, hammering in the underground adits.   If they hear them now, it is because they have heard from their grandsires that such underground Little People did work. There exist many ancient mines in which iron tools are found.   They never extend very far.   But they afford proof that at some remote period there were miners by profession, hereditary miners maybe, of a different stock from those who are now engaged in the same work.

In Cornwall the stories of the Little Folk workers in mines have passed from those who sought iron ore to those who followed the veins of tin.   But there miners often see them.   Mr Hunt says: 'A tinner told my informant that he had often seen them sitting on pieces of timber, or tumbling about in curious attitudes, when he came to work.

Miners do not like the form of the cross being made underground. A friend of my informant, going through some levels or adits, made a × by the side of one, to know his way back, as he would have to return by himself. He was compelled to alter it into another form.' This is interesting, as everywhere the Dwarfs are regarded as hostile to Christianity, and are represented in many places as migrating because they cannot endure the sound of church bells calling to prayer. Who first sought out the veins of iron? Who but such as had known where to find it, and what its characteristics were as ore? The natives of the Caucasus were the originators of steel manufacture, but the art was acquired from them by other tribes.

The working in iron, and in consequence the mining for iron, seems in former times, and to a certain extent to the present day, to be specialised in particular tribes. It is so in Africa. There are tribes whose whole energies are devoted thereto. Neighbouring tribes knew nothing about the process. They buy ready-made weapons and tools of these ironworkers.

In Ceylon and India the steel manufacture is confined to certain classes. For the perfecting of a good blade, infinitely hard and

flexible, the smith will devote an amount of
labour and time which we should think
thrown away. He tempers the blade in
oil not twenty or thirty times, but twice that
amount, till he is satisfied that it has attained
the perfection he desires. When we read in
the Scandinavian Sagas of the digging into
old grave-mounds in quest of swords that had
been manufactured by Dwarfs, we are forced
to the conviction that such blades, if good for
anything, must have been thus oil-tempered
again and again in the manufacture, and so
only could have withstood rust.

The knowledge of iron came to the Greeks
about 1200 B.C., and iron weapons and
implements were carried up the Danube by
Scythian nomadic dealers. A great centre of
early iron manufacture would seem to have
been in Illyria and Thrace, but who the
ironworkers were who travelled in the north
of Europe and in Britain we do not know.

A few characteristic stories of this people
must suffice. A man rode one morning on
the way from Apenrade to Jordkirch by the
'Three hills.' He heard hammering going
on vigorously in one. So he shouted that
he wanted a chaff-cutter, and rode on his
way. In the evening, on his return, he saw
a brand-new chaff-cutting knife lying on the

side of the hillock.  He put down its value and
carried it off.  It proved to be of unwonted
sharpness, but also that a cut or wound dealt
by it never healed.  On the estate of Dollrott,
in Schleswig, when one lies down on a green
tumulus that exists there, one can hear
work going on underground.  It is the same
with the Great Struchberg near Heiligenhafen,
when one places an ear to the ground the
hammering at a smithy can be heard.

It seems to be a general opinion that the
Little People must be treated with fairness,
that any act of treachery done to them or
neglect is bitterly resented.

Two serving-girls in Tavistock said that
the pixies were very kind to them, and would
drop silver for them into a bucket of clean
water, which they took care to place for
them in the chimney-corner every night.
Once it was forgotten, and the pixies forth-
with went up to the girls' room and loudly
complained of the neglect.  One of them,
who happened to be awake, jogged the other,
and proposed going down to rectify the
omission, but she said, 'for her part she
would not stir out of bed to please all the
pixies in Devonshire.'  The other went down
and filled the bucket, in which, by the way,
she found next morning a handful of silver

pennies.  As she was returning, she heard the
pixies debating how they might punish the
other, and they agreed to give her a lame leg
for a term of seven years, then to be cured
by a herb growing on Dartmoor, whose
name of seven syllables she could not recall.
Next morning, Molly, the lazy wench, arose
dead lame, and so continued till the end of the
period, when, one day, as she was picking up
a mushroom a strange-looking boy started up
and insisted on *striking* her leg with a plant
which he held in his hand.  He did so, and
she was cured, and became the best dancer
in the town.

The people of Jutland declare that when
God cast the rebellious angels out of heaven,
some fell down on the mounds or barrows and
became Hill-folk; others fell into the elf-moors
and became Elf-folk; and others, again, fell
into dwellings and became House-kobolds.
This gives a rough idea of the distinction
supposed to exist among these Little People.

The enormous number of traditions that
tell of the brownies, kobolds, or pixies doing
service in houses and farms point to a reminiscence of when this dispersed and unsettled
Little People did great help to farmers and
their wives for some small recompense.

One feature attends all the stories about

them—the love of independence they possessed, their intolerance at being watched.

In the early part of the nineteenth century there were numerous dwarfs called Heinzelmen who did all sorts of work in the city of Cologne. They baked bread, washed, and did any sort of domestic labour, for which they expected to be paid with a bowl of sweet milk, into which white bread had been broken. At that time there were many bakers who kept no apprentices, for the Little People used always to make overnight as much black and white bread as the bakers wanted for their shops; and in many households they scoured the coppers, swept the hearths, and washed up the utensils for the maids. This went on till a tailor's wife, who had been especially favoured by the Heinzelmen, overcome with curiosity, resolved on having a peep at them. Accordingly she strewed peas up and down the stairs, so that they might fall and hurt themselves, and she might get a sight of them next morning. But the project missed, and since that time the Heinzelmen have totally disappeared.

They can also be driven away by one being over-generous to them.

In Scotland the brownie is the same as the German kobold and the Devonshire pixy:

a personage of small stature, wrinkled visage,
and wearing a brown mantle and hood.  His
residence is in the hollow of an old tree,
a ruined castle, or the abode of man.  He
is attached to certain families, with whom he
has been known to reside, even for centuries,
threshing the corn, cleaning the house, doing
everything done by his English, German,
and Scandinavian brethren.  He expects to
be paid with a bowl of cream, or some fresh
honeycomb, laid for him in a corner.

A good woman had just made a web of
linsey-woolsey, and prompted by her kindly
nature, had manufactured from it a mantle
and hood for her little brownie.  Not content
with laying the gift in one of his favourite
spots, she indiscreetly called to tell him it
was there.  This was too direct, and brownie
quitted the place, crying,—

'A new mantle, and a new hood;
Poor Brownie! ye'll ne'er do mair gude!'

Versions of this story are found everywhere,
where these Little People have been supposed
to help.  Altogether another form of the
incident is in *The Mad Pranks and Merry
Jests of Robin Goodfellow*, that appeared
before 1588.

Coming to a farmer's house, he takes a
liking to a 'good handsome maid' that was

there, and in the night does her work for her
at breaking hemp and flax, bolting meal, etc.
Having watched one night and seen him at
work, and observed that he was rather bare
of clothes, she provided him with a waist-
coat against the next night.  But when he
saw it, he started and said :—

> Because thou layest me hempen hempen,
> I will neither bolt nor stampen :
> 'Tis not your garments, new or old,
> That Robin loves; I feel no cold.
> Had you left me milk or cream,
> You should have had a pleasing dream;
> Because you left no drop or crumb,
> Robin never more will come.

Where a condition of affairs existed connected with a people of foreign race, misunder-
stood, looked on with superstitious fears,
whose very ways encouraged mistrust, it is
no wonder that stories concerning them
should be wild and fantastic.  Not only so—
but that many a myth connected with beings
pertaining to a religion superseded by
Christianity was certain to adhere to them and
assist in making them nebulous and extrava-
gant ; that is what one would expect to take
place.  Have any burials of this people been
discovered?  I will not say that they have
not ; but they have not been discriminated,
not looked for.

In September, 1900, I received a summons
to go to Padstow in Cornwall, as at Harlyn
Bay near there a prehistoric necropolis had
been discovered in blown sand that had
been carried some way inland and was hard
compacted.   A gentleman had bought a field
there, and was about to build a house.   I found
that he was impatient to get his dwelling
ready before winter, or, at all events, have
the foundations and walls got on with, and
he would not allow a slow and a careful
exploration.   It had to be done in a hurry.
What was more, and even worse, the fact
of the discovery got into the Cornish and
Devon papers.   The season was that of tourists.
The owner charged sixpence a head for
visitors, and they came in swarms, pushing
everywhere, poking about the skeletons and
skulls with their umbrellas and parasols,
scrabbling in the graves in quest of 'finds,'
and from the moment this rabble appeared
on the scene no work could be done save protection of what had already been uncovered.
A more distressing and disappointing exploration could not be imagined.   However, some
points were determined.

More than a hundred graves were uncovered ; they were composed of boxes of
slate in which the skeleton sat crouched,

mainly, but not exclusively, on the right side.
Some were of females, some of mothers with
their infants in their arms.   No skull was
discovered that indicated death through
violence, and all skeletons were complete.
Some of the coffins were in layers, one above
another; rudely speaking, they pointed east
and west, the heads being to the west; but
what governed the position seemed to be
the slope of the hill, that fell away somewhat
steeply from the south to the north.

Some bronze fibulæ were found, finely
drawn armlets of bronze wire making spiral
convolutions about the wrist, a necklace of
very small amber and blue glass beads strung
on thin bronze wire; a good deal of iron so
corroded that, what with the friability and
the meddlesomeness of the visitors, who would
finger everything exhumed, it was not possible
to make out more than that they did not
represent fragments of weapons.

The fibulæ were exhibited in London by
Mr Charles H. Read, and described in the
*Proceedings of the Society of Antiquaries*,
vol. xxi., pp. 272–4.  They are of the crossbow
type, not British, their nearest analogues are
found in the Iberian Peninsula.  The pin
of the brooch was perfect when found, but
not so when Mr Read saw it, and he wrongly

describes it. He considered the Harlyn
interments to date from about the third
century B.C.

There were found at the time a great many
needles and prongs of slate, which were afterwards exhibited on the spot and sold to
tourists as stone spear-heads. They were
no such thing. They were splinters of a soft
local slate that had been rolled by the wind
and grated by the sand into the shape they
assumed, and such are found all through the
district.

Dr Beddoe came down and examined the
skulls and skeletons. He considered the
interments to be late, and of a race somewhat
short in stature, with dolichocephalic skulls,
not prognathous. 'We may conjecture with
some confidence that it was after the Gallo-
Belgic and before the Roman Conquest.'
There were marked peculiarities in the skulls,
distinguishing them from those of the Aryan
Celt and from those of the men of the Bronze
period. It seemed to me to be a necropolis
of an intrusive people, peaceable, who, whereas
all around them burnt their dead, continued
religiously to inter theirs.

The main road from Padstow along the
coast cuts through this ancient cemetery.
It is interesting to note that this portion of

the road has ever been dreaded by passengers at night as haunted. On the right hand of the way, coming from Padstow, probably more of the necropolis remains, and it is earnestly to be desired that it may at some time be scientifically examined, without the intrusion of the ignorant and vulgar being permitted. The digging proceedings at Harlyn, as soon as the season was ending, were broken up by a storm and change of weather. The tent was blown down and utterly wrecked. In the following year no opportunity was accorded for the prosecution of the researches.

I think that the Harlyn exploration affords sufficient grounds to make antiquaries careful in examining graves, and caution in classification in the broad categories of prehistoric, Celtic, Saxon, and Roman.

To what stock an intrusive people—widely dispersed and never collected into towns, villages, or hamlets, but migrating through the land, like the gipsies—belonged is what cannot yet be determined.

## CHAPTER X

### BIRTH AND MARRIAGE

I HAVE mentioned elsewhere[1] the strong
objection I found was entertained in Yorkshire
against having a child baptized in a new
font in a new church, the deeply-rooted conviction being that such a child became the
perquisite of the devil.

A like prejudice exists against being the
first person to cross the threshold of a new
house, as it is supposed that ill-luck, probably death, will ensue to him or her who
either daringly or unwittingly does so enter
a house for the first time. I am not sure that
the practice of asking some stranger to cut the
first sod, and making of that an honour, is
not an ingenious way devised of passing on
the ill-luck that would have fallen on one
engaged on the undertaking for which the
sod has to be cut, to another person ignorant
of what it entails. We had in Devonshire an
addition made to our churchyard, to which,
as on a lower level, descent had to be made
by a flight of steps. The utmost repugnance
was felt by the villagers to have one of their
dear ones be the first laid in it. At last a

[1] *Strange Survivals.* Methuen & Co.

poor gipsy boy died and was buried in the
new ground, and since then the dread has
been dispelled.

These superstitious fears of being the first
to pass over a new bridge, enter a new house,
be baptized in a new font, be laid in a
new cemetery, are very widely spread.   The
bronze valve of the doors of Aachen Cathedral
has a crack in it.   The story goes that the
town could not get the church built without
the assistance of the devil, who found sufficient
gold for the purpose on condition that he
should be given the first who passed into the
church when completed.   But as the news of
the conclusion of the compact got wind, no
one would enter.   So a trick was devised.
A wolf was caught, and on Sunday, when the
bells rang for service and a crowd was
assembled before the gates, the wolf was
let loose and dashed into the sacred building.
The devil came down in a whirlwind, laid
hold of his prey, but, seeing how he had been
balked, dashed the brazen doors together
with such violence that one split, and the
rent is visible to this day.   In commemoration
of what had occurred, a brazen wolf was
cast and planted by the doors.   In 1815 this,
which had been carried off to Paris by the
French, was returned and replaced.

The builder of the Sachsenhäuser bridge at Frankfort had engaged to get it completed by a certain day; but when two days off from that stipulated he found a couple of arches were still short of being finished, and in his despair called on the devil to assist him. The Evil One undertook to accomplish the work if given the first to traverse the bridge. He was disappointed by the builder driving a cock over. In his fury the devil broke two holes in the bridge that have never since been filled up. In commemoration of the incident, a gilt cock on an iron rod stands on the spot. upon the bridge.

The Devil's Bridge, near Aberystwyth, is over the Afon Mynach. The bridge has been thrown across a chasm 114 feet above the first fall, and 324 feet above the bottom of the cataract. Tradition tells—

> Old Megan Llandunach of Pont-y-Mynach
>   Had lost her only cow;
> Across the ravine the cow was seen,
>   But to get it she could not tell how.

In this dilemma the Evil One appeared to her cowled as a monk, and offered to cast a bridge across the chasm if she would promise him the first living being that should pass over it when completed. To this she gladly consented.

The bridge was thrown across the ravine, and the Evil One stood beyond bowing and beckoning to the old woman to come over and try it. But she was too clever to do that. She had noticed his left leg whilst he was engaged in the construction, and saw that the knee was behind in place of in front, and for a foot he had a hoof.

> In her pocket she fumbled, a crust out tumbled;
>   She called her little black cur;
> The crust over she threw, the dog after it flew,
>   Says she, 'The dog is yours, crafty sir!'

Precisely the same story is told of St Cadoc's Causeway, in Brittany. All these stories derive from one source, that it was held necessary to offer a sacrifice when either a house or a bridge or any public building was erected. The usual way was to lay the victim under the foundation stone. I have dealt with this subject already, so that I will but touch on it here. In the ballad of the *Cout of Keeldar*, in the minstrelsy of the Border, it is said,—

> And here beside the mountain flood
>   A mossy castle frowned,
> Since first the Pictish race in blood
>   The haunted pile did found.

In a note Sir Walter Scott alludes to the tradition that the foundation stones of Pictish raths were bathed in human gore.

But we are drifting away from the point specially to be considered—the sacrifice of the first-born, for this is what really the dim superstition amounts to that shrinks from allowing a child of one's own to be the first to be baptized in a new font or the first to be buried in a new cemetery.

The conviction that the first-born child had to be sacrificed is very ancient. We see it in Genesis, where Abraham takes Isaac to Moriah, and in the subsequent redemption of the first-born by an offering to Jehovah. This was a belief or practice borrowed by the Hebrews from the Canaanitish inhabitants of the land.

The excavations of Tel-el-Hessy have revealed great numbers of infant bones, often in pots, buried under the platform on which rise some rude stone monoliths, and these were in all probability the first-born children of a family sacrificed to Baal.

In Exod. xiii. 2 is the command : 'Sanctify unto Me all the first-born, whatsoever openeth the womb among the children of Israel, both of man and of beast : it is Mine.' The first-born became *sacer*, not sacred only but destined to be sacrificed, and the first-born child had to be redeemed at a price, whereas the first-born of cattle had to die. 'The

first-born of thy sons shalt thou give unto Me.
Likewise shalt thou do with thine oxen and
with thy sheep' (Exod. xxii. 29–30). But
then came the concession : 'All the first-
born of thy sons shalt thou redeem' (Exod.
xxxiv. 20). Among the Canaanites, so far as
we know, there was no redemption; and
perhaps the concession to the usages of
the heathen around, with the way shown by
which escape might be had from a barbarous
custom, was allowed so as to introduce among
the Canaanites a mitigation of a horrible
usage. When Jephtha went to fight against
the children of Ammon, he vowed to sacrifice
the first living being that he met on his
return from battle; and as this was his
daughter, he was compelled to fulfil his vow
by immolating her.

I do not myself think that the sacrifice of
the first-born, or the first of any being, or the
burial of a human victim under a foundation
stone, was of Aryan origin, although Aryans
may have adopted such a usage from those
of another race whom they overlay. The
notion of burying under foundations is very
prevalent in India and throughout the East,
among the Dravidian and Malay peoples,
but to the best of my knowledge is not
indigenous among the Hindus.

A superstition I found common in Yorkshire was that, where several children were to be baptized at the same time, it would be fatal to take a girl before a boy—for by so doing the girl would acquire a beard and moustache, and the boy grow up smooth-faced. Whence that notion arose I cannot say. This belief is not confined to Yorkshire, it is found in Durham, and extends as far north as the Orkney Isles.

The first visit made by a baby to another house is an occasion for its receiving an egg, salt, white bread, and in the East Riding of Yorkshire, some matches. These are pinned into the child's long clothes; and several of my children have received these gifts. With the egg comes the promise of immortality, or else of the child itself becoming a parent; the salt signifies salubrity of mind and body; the white bread a promise of having all things needful during life; and, finally, the matches are to light the child on its way to heaven.

I come now to a matter in connection with the social and moral development of the British people that must be dealt with, although it is one to be touched on as lightly as may be. St Jerome says that he had met the Attacotti, inhabitants of our isles, who were barbarians, having their wives in

common. I do not see that we can reject
his testimony, though it concerns, I am convinced, not the Aryan invaders, but the
original inhabitants of the isles. And there
is something to bear out his statement. We
know very little about the Picts, but the
consensus of opinion is that they were a pre-
Aryan people. And we have the succession
recorded of the Pictish kings. From this we
learn that the kingship descended through
the mothers; that, in fact, a matriarchate
existed. This in itself implies polyandry, and
among wild tribes this did exist to a large
extent. To the present day, in Tibet, a
woman belongs to several men. In Ceylon she
is the wife of perhaps three brothers; and when
one husband visits her, he leaves his staff
at the door to show that he is in possession.
At the present day, in England, an illegitimate
child bears the mother's name; and although
the father may be perfectly well known,
he has no rights over his issue, nor over the
property of the mother, which passes to her
own offspring.

In my neighbourhood there is a high ridge
of down, in a half-moon, in the lap of which
lie several villages. In my boyhood it was
quite possible to distinguish between the
villagers of two of these. Those in one were

blue-eyed, fair-haired, clear-skinned, upright, truthful, straightforward men, somewhat sluggish in temperament. But the others were dusky, high-cheekboned, with dark hair; tricky, unscrupulous, very energetic, and sadly immoral. The railways and excellent roads have tended to fuse the types; but, nevertheless, I could pick the distinct races out without difficulty at the present day. I do not say that the fair and evidently Aryan colonists were as moral as might be desired, but if there were a lapse, there was shame, whereas with the others there was none at all. The first were amenable to discipline and to spiritual influences; the others were quite beyond reach. Only where there was a fusion of blood was there any chance of amendment.

At an early period, where the woman belonged to several men, all rights to property and to succession to authority descended through the mother. There are tribes in which this is still the case.

But there came a great revulsion of feeling. The father at last determined to insist on his paternity, and polyandry practically ceased. In Britain, Christian legislation came in to assist the change; but as we shall see presently, where that did not exist, a most curious system was adopted to establish paternity.

In Tyrol, at the present day, so as not to break up an allodial farm, where there be, say, five brothers, on the death of the father lots are cast as to which of the brothers is to marry and continue the family. The lot does not always fall on the eldest; but however it falls, it is submissively obeyed. In a farm one may see the brothers working as common operatives, under the direction of the married brother. None of them think of marrying—their lot is to remain on the allodial land and work for it.

But this points back to a prior condition of affairs, when the woman was the wife of all the brothers, as is the condition now in Ceylon. Christianity has stepped in and altered that; and now these simple, honest, pure-minded men work on humbly and lovingly under the direction of their brother and sister-in-law.

And now we come to the method adopted among a wild people to establish paternity in place of matriarchy, and that was the couvade.

Mr Tylor has dealt with this, and has shown how that among an uncultured people the idea exists that the health of the child is inseparably bound up with that of the parent.

But he has not shown—what I think is the most important point of all—*why* the nursing of the baby and the going to bed was transferred to the father from the mother. I will quote just a few examples, and then explain my theory.

About eighteen hundred years ago Strabo informed his readers that among the Iberians, in Northern Spain, the women, 'after the birth of a child, tend their husbands, putting them to bed instead of going themselves,' and this practice still continues among the modern Basques. 'In Biscay,' says Michel, 'in valleys whose population recalls the usages of society in its infancy, the women rise immediately after child-birth and attend to the duties of the household, while the husband goes to bed, taking the baby with him, and thus receives the neighbours' compliments.' The same usage has been found also in Navarre, as well as on the French side of the Pyrenees. The Tiboreni of Pontus, to the south of the Black Sea, once practised the couvade. Among them, when the child was born, the father took to his bed with his head tied up and lay groaning, whilst the mother tended him with soup and bread, and prepared his taths. In the old French Lai of *Aucassin and Nicolette*, in its present

form of the latter half of the thirteenth
century, Aucassin arrives at the palace of
the King of Torelore and finds him 'au lit
et en couche,' whereupon he takes a stick
to his majesty, turns him out of bed, and
makes him promise to abolish this absurd
custom in his realm. The couvade prevailed
also in Corsica. It is not in Europe alone
that the couvade existed. It is found still
in Borneo; in a tribe subjected to the Chinese
Empire; in Africa; and among the peoples
of America, in Brazil, and among the Caribs.

'The peoples,' says Mr Tylor, 'who have
kept it up in Asia and Europe seem to have
been not the great progressive, spreading,
conquering, civilising nations of the Aryan,
Semitic, and Chinese stocks. It cannot be
ascribed even to the Tartars, for the Lapps,
Finns, and Hungarians appear to know
nothing of it. It would rather seem to have
belonged to that ruder population, or series
of populations, whose fate it has been to be
driven by the great races out of fruitful lands
to take refuge in mountains and deserts.'[1]

In primitive society the women were the
property of the men, and one woman was
often enough the property of several men,

[1] Tylor (E. B.). *Early History of Mankind.* Lond.,
1865, p. 297.

or else the women of a tribe belonged to the
entire tribe, and no child could say who was
his father.    Indeed, the woman could not
identify the father of her child.    Consequently
there was a stage in society in which the
children were related to their mother only.
M'Lennan says of the Australian aborigines:
'It is not in quarrels uncommon to find
children of the same father arrayed against
one another, or, indeed, against the father
himself, for by their peculiar law the father
can never be a relative to his own children.'
This can arise only out of a still earlier stage
of society, when the women were the common
property of the tribe, so that the fathers of
the children were not known.    The institution
of the couvade marks a revolt against this
horrible condition of affairs, and indicates a
moral change, when the father was resolved
to insist on his own parentage and property
in the child.    It was, in a word, the rebellion
against promiscuity and the beginning of the
family.

But how was the father to assert his
paternity?    Only by pretending to be confined of the babe, showing by every possible
exhibition of debility, and exhaustion, and
by solicitude in eating and drinking only
such things as could not hurt the child, as if

he were actually suckling it. That was the curious method adopted to escape to a higher social stage. If among the Semitic and Aryan peoples there is found no trace of the couvade, it is because these peoples never did emerge from a social state in which the family did not exist, in which the patriarchate was not recognised, and recognised as the great social basis.

I will now take up another point. It may be noticed how that in most of our nursery tales relating to the adventures of several brothers it is always the youngest who comes out topmost.

The typical story is the White Cat. A king sends his three sons forth, promising to bestow the kingdom on him who shall present him with the smallest dog. This the youngest produces; then he subjects them to a fresh trial—he will confer the crown on him who can procure lawn so fine as to be drawn through a needle's eye. Again the third son succeeds. The last trial is—succession to the throne is to be accorded to him who brings back the most beautiful princess. Again, and finally, the youngest triumphs, as he produces the White Cat transformed into a most miraculously beautiful damsel.

Generally, in the similar stories, the elder

brothers are jealous and seek to rob the youngest of his prize and attempt to murder him.

There are corresponding stories in Grimm's *Kinder Märchen*.  In the 'Water of Life' the old king is sick, and the sons go in quest of this water, and only the youngest finds it. On the way home the brothers rob him of it—but in the end all turns out well.

Here is in brief a modern Greek household tale.  A king had three sons and a mirror, by looking into which an enemy might be seen meditating mischief.  In a high gale the magic mirror was carried away and could not be found ; accordingly the three princes set out to endeavour to recover it.  At a point in the road there diverged three ways.  Each laid his ring at this place, and all agreed to meet there at the termination of a given time.  The eldest went one way, squandered his money in riotous living, and was so reduced that he had to become an ox-driver.  The second did likewise, and to obtain a livelihood herded swine.  The third went on till he came to the cottage of an old woman who took him in, and who had a beautiful daughter.  As he saw that she was a knowing old person, he told her what his quest was, and she informed him that the mirror hung in an apple tree

in the garden of a drake. If he would obtain
it he must remove the mirror without letting
fall an apple. However, in his efforts to
obtain what he desired, he disturbed one of
the fruit, which fell, whereupon the mirror
cried out, 'I am being stolen !' The prince
had the utmost difficulty in escaping with
his life. He returned to the old woman, who
told him he must abide a twelvemonth before
making a second attempt. In the meantime
he fell in love with the daughter. His second
venture being successful, he rode homewards,
taking his bride behind him on his horse.
Arrived at the spot where the rings had
been deposited, he learned what had befallen
his brothers, so he paid their debts, freed them,
and brought them away with him. They
became envious, and when he was asleep flung
him into a river. Happily he managed to
escape, and going into the town apprenticed
himself to a gold embroiderer and became
skilful in the art. Meanwhile the brothers
had gone to the king, their father, given him
the mirror, and the elder resolved on marrying
the lady. The youngest contrived to send
her a letter, bidding her obtain her wedding
trousseau only from him. Accordingly,
when she was being provided with wedding
garments she rejected all, and declared she

would wear no other gown than one she had
procured for herself. She then sent the
commission to her bridegroom, and when a
superb dress arrived embroidered with gold
in a manner never seen before, the king
ordered the craftsman to be brought before
him. That done, he recognised his youngest
son. The whole story now came out; he had
the two elder executed, and conferred the
kingdom on the one who deserved it.

Similar stories abound in Albania, in
Wallachia, and among the Serbs. There are
several German variants; and forms of the
story are found in Lithuania, also among
the Scottish Highlands. Among the classic
Greeks one can see the idea of the pre-
eminence in luck of the youngest son in
Hesiod's story of Chronos and Zeus. In the
Biblical narrative of Joseph and his brethren,
these latter are envious of him, throw him
into a pit, and then sell him as a slave; and
he comes out as second in the kingdom after
Pharaoh, and they go crouching to him for
bread; but in this case the resemblance is
accidental only. It does not arise out of an
institution as do the others. That institution
is the making of the youngest son heir to
his father's lands and place. This remains
customary throughout much of Germany,

even where the Code Napoléon is in force, as
in Baden.  The elder sons are bought off, go
to America, or enter into trade, whereas the
youngest succeeds to the farm, the byre, and
whatever pertains to the farm.  That this
is of practical advantage I have had shown
me in Germany.  The lusty young men can
best shift for themselves if given a small sum
to start upon; and when the *bauer* is old and
unable to execute all the work on the land, his
youngest son is in the full vigour of life.
What is usually done is for the *bauer* to value
his estate, and he does it pretty arbitrarily,
and divides its value into portions, according
as he has sons and daughters.  Then he
gives to such as want to go and establish
homes for themselves the sum he has allotted,
and makes them sign an acquittance that
they make no further claim on the farm.
That the elder children are usually served
shabbily, and entertain a jealousy of the
youngest, is what might be anticipated, and
this reflects itself in such stories as those to
which I have referred.

Belief in changelings was very prevalent
in former times throughout Northern Europe.
If a mother was brought to bed of a puny
mis-shapen little creature, very unlike its
brothers and sisters, with some peculiarity

about it, she was sure to suppose that it was not her own child, but one substituted for it by the Little Underground Folk. In the Western Isles, to the present day, idiots are believed to be changelings. The only redress open to the parents is to place the imp on the beach, below high-water mark, when the tide is out, and pay no heed to its screams. Rather than allow her child to be drowned by the rising waters, the elfin mother will make her appearance, carry it away, and restore the child that has been stolen.

Another way, when a mother is convinced that there is a changeling in the cradle in place of her own child, is to heat a poker red hot and ram it down the infant's throat. If it be a fairy brat, the mother will come in at the moment and snatch it away. Again, another mode of testing what the squalling, unsightly imp is, is to throw it on the fire. It is far from improbable that there have been many cases of getting rid of babes that did no credit to their mothers by this means— she fully persuaded that the creature she treated in this barbarous manner was actually not her own.

A fine child at Caerlaverock, in Nithsdale, was observed on the second day after its birth, and before it had been baptized, to

have become fractious, deformed, and ill-
favoured. His yelling every night deprived
the whole family of rest; it bit at its mother's
breasts, and would lie still neither in the
cradle nor in the arms. The mother being one
day obliged to go from home, left it in the
charge of the servant girl. The poor lass
was sitting bemoaning herself : 'Were it nae
for thy girning face, I would knock the big,
winnow the corn, and grun the meal.' 'Lowse
the cradle-band,' said the child, 'and tent
the neighbours, and I'll work yere work.'
Up he started—the wind arose, the corn was
chopped, the outlyers were foddered, the
hand-mill moved round, as by instinct, and
the knocking-mill did its work with amazing
rapidity. The lass and the child then rested
and diverted themselves till, on the approach
of the mistress, it was restored to the cradle
and renewed its cries. The girl took the
mother aside and related to her what had
happened. 'What'll we do with the wee deil?'
asked the mother. 'I'll work it a pirn,'
replied the lass. At midnight the chimney-
top was covered up, and every chink and
cranny stopped. The fire was blown till it
was glowing hot, and the maid speedily
undressed the child and tossed him on to the
burning coals. He shrieked and yelled in the

most dreadful manner; and in an instant
the Fairies were heard moaning on every
side, and rattling at the windows, door, and
chimney. 'In the name of God, bring back
the bairn,' cried the lass. The window flew
up, the real child was laid on the mother's
lap, and the wee deil flew up the chimney
laughing.

In this—and there are scores of other
stories of the same character — one can
hardly doubt that the conclusion is fictitious,
and was added to soften the account of a real
murder of a babe that was objectionable in
appearance, manner, and habits.

That the Small People, who have been
called brownies, pixies, elves, kobolds, but
which really were a race of people living in
the north of Europe, did occasionally steal the
children of the Aryan settlers, is possible
enough. The gipsies are accused of doing the
same thing nowadays; and the Jews were
similarly accused in the Middle Ages.

I will pass on now to some marriage customs.
In the North, Skimmington, or Riding the
Stang, is illustrated by Rowlandson in *Dr
Syntax's Tour in Search of Consolation.*

A procession is formed of youths and
maidens, beating drums, rattling canisters
filled with pebbles, blowing trumpets, and

bearing stags' horns and cow horns on the
top of poles, with sheets or petticoats flying
below. This procession attends a man and
his wife seated back to back on an ass.

> 'Such a strange show I ne'er have seen,'
> Syntax exclaim'd, 'What can it mean?
> Patrick, you may perchance explain
> The hist'ry of this noisy train.'

> 'Please you,' Pat answered, 'I can tell
> This frolic-bus'ness mighty well :
> For there's no place I ever saw
> Where this is not the parish law.'

Patrick goes on to explain that it is the
punishment inflicted on a hen-pecked husband,
on one where the gray mare is the better
horse. But this is not the original and more
general signification, as the horns carried on
the rods indicate. It expressed the popular
feeling when the recognised code of honour
was broken. It attended marriages where
scandal attached to the union. Mr Henderson
says : 'The riding of the stang has been
practised from time immemorial in the towns
and villages of the North of England, and is
still resorted to on occasions of notorious
scandal. A boy or young man is selected,
placed on a ladder or pole, and carried
shoulder-height round the town, the people
who accompany him having armed themselves
with every homely instrument whence noise

can be extracted—poker and tongs, kettles and frying-pans, old tin pots, and so forth. Amid the discordant sounds thus produced, and the yells, cheers, and derisive laughter of the mob, the procession moves to the house of him whose misdeeds evoked it. At his door the rider recites in doggerel verse the cause of the disturbance, beginning—

'Hey derry! Hey derry! Hey derry dan!
It's neither for my cause nor your cause I ride the stang,
But for——

'The indictment is, of course, made as ludicrous as possible, and intermixed with coarse jests and mockery.'

Not many years ago the bride of a medical man in Yorkshire, thinking that her husband was too warmly attached to a servant maid who had been some time in his service, ran away to her father's house. Popular feeling was on her side, and the stang was ridden for some nights before the surgeon's door. The end was that he had to dismiss the servant, whereupon the wife returned to him.

In France the Charivari is much of the same character. In Devonshire it takes a different form, and always occurs on the wedding night of a couple who have caused some talk—but not by any means always

justly. It is called the Stag Hunt, and notice
is given of its coming off a few days before.
I copied one of these :—

> This is to give Notice,
> That on Saturday evening next, at 8 o'clock
> p.m., The Red Hunter will assemble his
> hounds at the Cross, and there will be
> a famous Stag Hunt.

On such an occasion a man personates the
stag, having horns attached to his head and
a bladder full of blood under his chin. The
huntsman wears a scarlet coat and blows
a horn, and the pack is made up of yelping,
barking boys. The hunt goes on up and
down the road with incredible noise, till at
last the stag is brought to bay on the doorstep of the newly-married pair, when the
huntsman stands astride over the fallen stag,
blows a furious blast, and proceeds to slit
the bladder with his knife and pour the blood
over the stone and threshold.

This has happened in my own immediate
neighbourhood at least seven times in the
last twenty years.

It is supposed to be the expression of out-
raged moral opinion ; but it has degenerated
into a performance on the occasion of any
marriage; and young people, if they can
possibly afford it, manage to flee the village
for a couple of days or more—not always

successfully, for the performance, if they be at all unpopular, is organised to salute them on their return.

In Devonshire, as a bride leaves the church an old woman presents her with a little bag containing hazel nuts. These have the same signification as rice, and betoken fruitfulness— the rice is undoubtedly a late substitution for hazel nuts. And now we have confetti of paper as substitute for rice, itself a substitute for nuts. Catullus tells us that among the ancient Romans newly-married people were given nuts. Among the Germans 'to go a-nutting' is a euphemism for love-making; and the saying goes that a year in which are plenty of nuts will also be one in which many children will be born.

The hazel nut would seem to have been a symbol of life. In a Celtic grave opened near Tuttlingen, in Würtemberg, in 1846, was found a body in a coffin made of a scooped-out tree with iron sword and bow, and a pile of fifteen hazel nuts. Another had in its hand a cherry stone, and between its feet thirty-two nuts.

On the wedding day the Romans cast nuts. Catullus refers to this usage. So does Virgil—

Sparge, marite, nuces; tibi descrit Hesperus Oetam.—*Bucol*, viii. **v. 80.**

At Gaillac, in France, they do not wait
the completion of the ceremony; for whilst
the young couple are still kneeling at the foot
of the altar, a rain of nuts is poured over their
heads and down their backs.  In the Gex, at
the ball which the bride is expected to give
on the day when her banns are published
for the first time, all the guests arrive with
nuts in both their hands wherewith to salute
her.  In Poitou the floor of the room where the
wedding breakfast is to be held is strewn with
nuts.  In the department of Hautes-Alpes
the bride, as she goes through the village, is
made to eat sugar plums made in the shape
of hazel nuts.

Wright, in his *Collection of Mediæval Latin
Stories*, has this : 'I have seen in many places,
when women get married, and are leaving
the church and returning home, that corn is
thrown in their faces with cries of "Abundantia !  Abundantia !" that in French is
*Plente, plente*; and yet very often before the
year is out they have remained poor and
beggars, and deficient in abundance of all
good things.'

In the Jura, acorns are scattered in place
of nuts or corn.

The casting of the old shoe signifies the
surrender of authority by the father to the

husband of his daughter. In some French provinces, when the bride is about to go to church, all her old shoes have been hidden away. In Roussillon it is always the nearest relative to the bridegroom who puts on her shoes, and these are new. The meaning comes out clearer in Berry, where all the assistants try to put the bride's shoes on, but fail, and it is only the bridegroom who succeeds. It was also a custom in Germany for the old shoes to be left behind, and new shoes given by the bridegroom to be assumed. A harsher way in Germany was for him to tread hard on the bride's foot, to show that he would be master.

In Scandinavia, if a man desired to adopt a son he slaughtered an ox, had the hide taken off from the right leg, and a shoe made out of it. This shoe the man first drew on, and then passed it on to his adopted son, who also put his foot into it. This indicated that he had passed under the authority of the father. When in the Psalm the expression occurs, 'Over Edom have I cast out My shoe,' the meaning is that Jehovah extended His authority over Edom. And when we say that a man has stepped into his father's shoes, we mean that the authority, position, and consequence of the parent has been transferred to his son.

When Ruth's kinsman refused to marry her, and resigned all authority and rights over her, 'as it was the custom in Israel concerning redeeming and concerning changing, a man plucked off his shoe and delivered it to his neighbour' (Ruth iv. 7, 8).

In Yorkshire, in some parts it is the custom to pour a kettleful of boiling water over the doorstep just after the bride has left her old home; and they say that before it dries up another marriage is sure to be agreed on. But I have seen in Devonshire the doorstep well scrubbed with water and soap directly the bride has left; and this was to wash away the impress of her foot, and show that the old home was to be no more a home to her, as she had chosen another.

Another symbolical act indicative of a change of life is the placing of a bench or stool at the church door, over which the bride and bridegroom are constrained to leap.

I have several times in Yorkshire seen at a wedding a race for a ribbon. Properly speaking, it should be the bride's garter which is claimed. She stands at the winning-post, and the lads race to see who can reach her first and get the ribbon and a kiss. But the ribbon is a substitute for the garter, provided by the bridegroom; the usage dates back to a remote and particularly barbarous antiquity. The girl belonged to her tribe, and the bridegroom could not obtain her as his wife without resistance from the youths of the tribe, and buying them off. In France and in Flanders it existed, and exists still. It was even forbidden by a Council held at Milan as late as 1586. In France the girl who married out of her village, on leaving its confines, flung back at the pursuing youths a ball of wool containing a piece of silver money, and whilst they struggled and fought for its possession she made her escape. At the present day a ribbon is extended across her path, and she pays a fee to have it lowered and let her go her way. Formerly the struggle to obtain the bride's garter took place directly after the nuptial benediction, and Brand, in his *Popular Antiquities*, gives an account of it. But the bride usually gave it away herself, and it was cut into small pieces.

Mr Henderson gives an account of some wild proceedings that take place at a wedding in the North of England. He says: 'I am informed by the Rev. J. Barmby that a wedding in the Dales of Yorkshire is indeed a thing to see; that nothing can be imagined comparable to it in wildness and obstreperous mirth. The bride and bridegroom may possibly be a little subdued, but their friends are like men bereft of reason. They career round the bridal party like Arabs of the desert, galloping over ground on which, in cooler moments, they would hesitate even to walk a horse—shouting all the time, and firing volleys from the guns they carry with them. . . . In the higher parts of Northumberland, as well as on the other side of the Border, the scene is, if possible, still more wild.'

The custom of firing guns when accompanying the bride is very widely distributed, and I have seen the same in the Pyrenees and in Bavaria.

This is a relic of a very early usage, when the bride was carried away by a lover; and very often among savage tribes the attempt at bride-capture was made when she was being about to be given away to one of her own stock.

# BIBLIOGRAPHY

[It is impossible to do more than give a selection of works on Folk-lore: they have of late years become very numerous.]

AUBREY, J. *Gentilism and Judaism.* 1686–1687 ; reprint, 1881.

BARING-GOULD, S. *Strange Survivals.* 1892.

BASSETT, F. S. *Legends of the Sea, etc.* 1885.

BLACK, W. G. *Counting-out Rhymes.* 1888.

BROWNE, SIR THOMAS. *Popular Errors.* 1646 ; reprint, 1852.

*CHAMBERS, R. *The Book of Days.* 2 Vols. 1864.

*Choice Notes from Notes and Queries (Folk-lore).* 1859.

CLOUSTON, W. A. *Popular Tales, etc.* 2 Vols. 1887.

FELIX-FAURE-GOYAN. *La Vie et la Mort des Fees.* 1910.

FRAZER, J. G. *The Golden Bough.* One Volume Edition.

FRAZER, J. G. *Totemism.* 1887.

FROBENIUS, L. *The Childhood of Man.* 1909.

GOMME, G. L. *Ethnology of Folk-lore.* 1896.

GOMME, G. L. *Handbook of Folk-lore.* 1890.

GOMME, G. L. *Folk-lore as a Historical Science.* 1908.

GOMME, G. L. *Folk-lore Relics of Early Village Life.* 1883.

GRIMM, J. L. C. *Deutsche Mythologie.* 2 Vols. 1835, 1847. English Translation, 4 Vols., 1880–1888.

HARTLAND, E. S. *Science of Fairy Tales.* 1891.

HASLITT, W. C. *Faiths and Folk-lore.* 2 Vols. 1905.

*HONE, W. *Everyday Book, Year Book, and Table Book.* 7 Vols. 1826–1832.

KELLY, W. R. *Curiosities of Indo-European Tradition.* 1863.

KEIGHTLY, T. *The Fairy Mythology.* 1828. New Ed. Bohn, n.d.

KEIGHTLY, T. *Popular Fictions.* 1834.

LANG, A.  *Custom and Myth.*  1884.

MANNHARDT, W.  *Germanische Mythen.*  1858.

MANNHARDT, W.  *Die Göttez d. Deutschen u. Nord. Völkes.*  1860.

MANNHARDT, W.  *Wald u. Feld Kulte.*  2 vols.  1875–1877.

NORK, F.  *Mythologie d. Volks Sagen.*  1848.

NORK, F.  *Sitten u. Getrüuche.*  1849.

TYLER, E. B.  *Primitive Culture.*  2 Vols.  3rd Ed.  1891

THORPE, B.  *Mythology and Popular Traditions.*  8 Vols..  1851.

### AMERICAN

BRINTON, D. G.  *Myths of the New World.*  1868.  New Ed., 1896.

DERMAN, R. M.  *Origin of Primitive Superstitions.*  1881.

MULLER, J. G.  *Geschichte d. Am. religion.*  1855.

### ENGLISH

BRAND, J.  *Observations on Popular Antiquities.*  1813.  3 Vols.  Various Editions.

BRAY, A. E.  *The Tamar and the Tavy : Traditions, etc., of Devon.*  8 Vols.  1838.  In 2 vols., New Ed., 1879.

HARDWICK, C.  *Traditions, etc., of Lancashire, etc.*  1872.

HARLAND, J., and WILKINSON, T. T.  *Lancashire Folk-lore.*  1867.

HENDERSON, W.  *Folk-lore of the Northern Counties.*  2nd Edition.  1879.

HUNT, R.  *Popular Romances of the West of England.*  2 Series.  1865, 1881.

JACKSON, G. F.  *Shropshire Folk-lore.*  1883.

MOORE, A. W.  *Folk-lore of the Isle of Man.*  1891.

PARKINSON, T.  *Yorkshire Legends, etc.*  2 Series.  1888–1889.

ROBY, J.  *Popular Traditions of England and Lancashire.*  3 Vols.  1841.

THISELTON-DYER, *English Folk-lore.*  1878.

### SCOTTISH

*County Folk-lore.*  Vol. 8.  1903.

CUNNINGHAM, A.  *Traditional Tales.*  1874.

DOUGLAS, G.  *Scottish Fairy and Folk Tales.*  1893.

GREGOR, W. *Notes on the Folk-lore of N.-E. Scotland.* 1881.

MACKINLAY, J. M. *Folk-lore of Scottish Lochs, etc.* 1893.

NAPIER, J. *Folk-lore.* 1879.

## IRISH

CROKER, T. CROFTON. *Fairy Legends and Traditions of the South of Ireland.* 1862. New Ed., Tegs, n.d.

CURTIN, J. *Tales of Fairies, etc.* 1895.

DEENY, D. *Peasant Lore.* 1900.

KENNEDY, P. *Legendary Fictions.* 1866.

LARMINIE, W. *Western Irish Folk Tales, etc.* 1893.

LOVER, S. *Legends, etc.* 2 Series. 1831–1837.

O'HANLON, J. *Irish Local Legends.* 1896.

RHYS, J. *Celtic Folk-lore.* 2 vols. 1901.

WILDE, J. *Ancient Cures, Charms, etc.* 1890.

WILDE, J. *Irish Fairy and Folk Tales.* N.d.

WOOD-MARTIN. *Traces of Elder Faiths.* 2 Vols. 1902.

## WELSH

JOHNS, G. *Legends, etc.* 1903.

RHYS, J. *Celtic Folk-lore.* 2 Vols. 1901.

SIKES, W. W. *British Goblins.* 1880.

## PERIODICALS AND SOCIETIES

*Folk-lore*, from 1890.

*Folk-lore Journal*, from 1883.

*Folk-lore Record*, from 1878.

*Melusine*, from 1878.

\**Notes and Queries*, from 1849.

*Zeitschrift d. Vereins f. Volkskünde*, from 1891.

\**The Proceedings and Journals of Various Archæological and other Societies in the Several Counties contain scattered up and down in them Notes on Folk-lore.*

\* Those so marked contain Notes on Folk-lore, together with other Matters Historical, Biographical, and Articles on Natural History

# INDEX